Hang the Little Man

Hang

THE LITTLE MAN

John Creasey

CHARLES SCRIBNER'S SONS
New York

CONTENTS

Hang the Little Man

I

EMPTY SHOP

MABEL STONE put the electric iron down on its end, brushed
back some damp hair from her forehead, and went slowly to
the open window which overlooked the little back yard, the
empty cartons standing by for collection when the next
wholesalers' delivery was made, the high brick wall, the narrow
gateway which had no gate. Beyond the wall and the service
passage behind it were the drab, smog-blackened houses of
Brittle Street, each three storeys high, each with a slate roof,
nearly all in need of painting.

Mrs. Klein's window box, nearly opposite this window, was
the one bright spot, aflame with scarlet geraniums; that fat old
German woman had a genius with flowers. Mabel did not
think beyond that, but at the back of her mind she knew that
Mrs. Klein had a genius for other things, too; for breaking
down the enmity and hostility of her neighbours during the
early days of the second world war, for instance. Mabel had
been a child then, but she could remember the wailing of
sirens and the frantic rush to the air raid shelters. Even more
vividly she remembered one night when the whole neighbourhood had gathered outside Mrs. Klein's, shouting, shaking
fists, going wild with rage because someone said that she had
shown a light to the German aeroplanes which had come to
bomb London. Mrs Klein, like her husband, had been
naturalised some time before the war began. She had lived
down all the hatred, and now people liked her, and did
many little kindnesses for her. She was in her seventies, had
been widowed for over ten years, and everyone loved the
colourful window boxes she had at the back as well as the
front. She was sitting there at her open window, thinking
about goodness know what, and her sharp old eyes must
have caught a movement at Mabel Stone's window, for she
waved.

Mabel, leaning out, waved back.

She wished it wasn't so hot, she wished Jim was back, she almost wished she wasn't going to have the baby. Although it was certain now, she could still hardly believe it; nine married-but-childless years had led her and Jim to believe they were going to be barren. She brushed the damp hair out of her eyes again, and began to smile, because it was ludicrous to wish the baby wasn't on the way; they were going to be so happy, so very, very happy.

It was the heat.

A stifling anticyclone had crept towards the British Isles a week ago, and was hovering over them; apart from one or two thunderstorms up and down the country, there had been blazing sun, fierce heat, and humid air which made movement an effort, and her body sticky. The only clean, clear thing in sight was the sky, so vivid a blue. A faint odour of wood smoke came from a garden some distance off, where garden clippings were being burned; that would be old Scrymegour—the man with the name she had never been able to pronounce, and still could not spell, although the Scrymegours had been customers here for at least forty years, since her parents had opened the shop. It was the only home she had ever known, and she had never consciously wanted a different one.

Jim was almost the only man she had ever known, certainly the only one she had known in passion and with love. Yet when she had first met him, she had been nervous of him, with his cultured voice and his superior manners. There had been some mystery, perhaps even tragedy in his life, although he had never said so; had simply told her that his father had died, leaving his mother and him penniless. Both had had to work; he had been selling wholesale groceries—and had called here.

Mabel could recall the glow in his eyes to this day; how he had stared at her.

He was out with the afternoon deliveries, and should be back by half past five; closing time. It was now just after five o'clock. The heat kept casual customers away, a lot of shop-

ping was done by telephone these days anyhow, and no one
had been in the shop for at least a quarter of an hour. Thursday was the dead, dull day of the week. Tomorrow the people
from the near neighbourhood would come in, starting in the
morning with the children bringing their mothers' orders on
the way to school.

With the baby, of course, they would have to have more
help, and in a way that wouldn't be a bad thing. Thursday
was the only day she spent here on her own; they had a
girl assistant for the rest of the week, but she wouldn't be any
use on her own. Jim had to be out much of the time, collecting
orders from further afield, and delivering; but they could
afford help. If Jim had a fault, it was being too tight with
money. He had a dread of growing old without having plenty
of capital by him; perhaps a legacy of his father's tragedy.

In a way, Mabel thought that he was more happy about the
baby even than she; he certainly intended to skimp nothing
that was needed for mother and child. Bless him! How she
wished he would step in now.

She heard the shop door bell ring, faintly.

She waited for the louder, clanging note which should
follow that first sound, but it did not come.

She stood up quickly, forgetting the heat and the recent
habit of clumsiness, for she was suddenly angry. The bell
would only ring on a muted note if someone was stopping it
from ringing—and she was almost sure who it was. Some of
the older, taller children of the neighbourhood, the little devils,
would sometimes sneak in, stretch over the counter for chocolate bars or wrapped sweets, and try to creep out without being
noticed. She knew at least two whom she would soon have to
report to their parents; but experience had taught Mabel
Stone that parents were often angry about their children being
"accused".

Mabel took two quick steps towards the half-closed door
which led into the shop. The door should be wide open, but it
always swung a little, and she had forgotten to prop it back.
She heard a movement, and at the same time, realised that she
mustn't let the sneak thieves know she was approaching; she

wanted to see who it was, but if they had the slightest warning they would run off before she could be sure. So she tip-toed towards the door. There were faint, furtive movements in the shop. She came within sight of the rows of canned fruit on the crowded shelves; every inch of space was used in this little gold-mine.

Mabel saw a slim figure, of a boy or a man wearing a dark jacket; but he wasn't simply stretching over the counter for easy-come chocolate and sweets, he was behind the counter, at the till. She heard a faint sliding noise, as the drawer opened, and realised that he had managed to stop the till bell from ringing, too. Her heart began to beat fast. The telephone was just inside the shop, so that they could answer it from the living-room when they were closed, and the possibility of dialling 999 sprang into her mind. It hovered. She stepped a little further into the shop itself, and saw the thief at the till, with his back towards her. He wasn't very tall, but was much more than a schoolboy. She saw him bring his hand from the till and thrust it into his pocket, and saw the crumpled pound and ten shilling notes. She could not stop herself from exclaiming:

"*What do you think you're doing?*"

At the first sound, he spun round, turning his small, lean, leathery face towards her. His thin lips were parted. She did not like the look of him. There was something vicious about his appearance; his very expression frightened her. Her lips began to quiver, and now she had to make herself say:

"*P—— put that money back.*"

She was close to the telephone, and moved her right hand towards it, but she was really too frightened to know what she was doing. The man was only a few feet away from her, glaring but unmoving. She lifted the telephone, and heard the faint *ting!* of the bell. As it came, she saw the man's right hand move swiftly. He snatched a tin of golden syrup from a pyramid on the counter, and with a movement so quick that she did not realise what he was going to do, he hurled the tin at her.

She felt a wild spasm of fear and thrust her hands up, to protect her face; but she was just too late. The heavy tin smashed into her right cheek. The pain was so awful that she could not even scream. Pain and terror drove away all thought of everything else, and tears of pain almost blinded her, but she caught a sight of the man leaping towards her. He was holding something else in his right hand, high above his head.

"No!" she gasped. "No!"

But he brought another tin down upon her head.

.   .   .   .

Jim Stone was whistling as he came away from Mrs. Jackson's, in Brittle Street, for hers was the last delivery of the day. He had been up to old Mrs. Klein already, and she had told him that his wife had been sitting at the living-room window. In her heavily accented voice, Mrs. Klein had asked:

"How iss she, Mr. Stone! She will be all right with the baby?"

"She's fine," Jim had assured her. "But it won't be for another three months yet."

"T'ree months, such a long time, such a short time." Mrs. Klein had a face so criss-crossed with lines that it looked like a mummy's, and her little eyes were bright and buried. "You look after her, Mr. Stone, your wife is a good, nice woman."

"Don't I know it," Jim had said, and laughed, and put the carton of groceries down in Mrs. Klein's kitchen. He noticed the small bar of chocolate which Mabel had pushed into the side; that was a habit of Mabel's with old customers and people of whom she was fond. If Mabel had a fault, it was being too free with money; and her parents had been the same. But who was he to grumble?

Mrs. Jackson was a middle-aged woman who had recently broken her leg, hence the delivery so close to the shop. He had no time for the big, flabby woman, and was glad that she hadn't wanted to talk. Now, whistling, he got into the Ford delivery van, with the wording on the sides reading:

M. & J. Stone
Grocers—Provisions.
Personal Service

painted in white on a red background. The van was immaculate inside and out; he and Mabel had cherished it as if it were a private car.

He switched on the engine, let in the clutch and eased the car into gear, then drove briskly but cautiously towards the corner. As he reached it, stopping to look both ways with extreme caution, he saw a man appear from the corner of Kemp Road—his road. This man glanced up and down, and then turned in the other direction and hurried away. This was peculiar, because only children hurried in heat like this. No one else was in sight, as it was a dead hour in the late afternoon, and Jim had time to watch the hurrying man, to see the way he looked over his shoulder as if he were afraid of being followed.

"Bit of an odd customer," he decided, and at once slowed down for his own corner, forgetting the man. He turned into Kemp Road, whistling again. His shop was on the far side. In the bright sunlight, the red of the fascia board looked dazzling, and the white lettering, in the same style as that on the van, stood out clearly. The door was closed and the blind down, just as the blind of the large window facing the street was down, to keep the shop cool in the slanting rays of the sun.

As Stone turned the corner of Middleton Street, a side turning off Kemp Road, he saw that the usual sign, reading *Open* by day, had been turned round, so that the *Closed* notice showed. At once he was full of alarm. Mabel couldn't be feeling well or she wouldn't have closed the shop; it was the heat, she had been complaining about it for days—Oh, gosh, Mabel was all right, wasn't she?

Instead of slowing down and turning into the service passage cautiously, Stone jammed on the brakes and jumped down; turning the van into the yard was a real work of art, and needed time. He saw no one as he ran along the passage, and was only subconsciously aware of the splash of red at Mrs. Klein's front window box. He swung round through the gateway—the gate had been removed so that the van could be taken in and out—and rushed to the back door. It was closed. The window was wide open, though, and he looked through into the small back room, with its two arm-chairs, the television set, a radio, some wooden chairs. He saw the ironing board in position and the iron standing on end, with a pile of folded clothes, looking fresh and brightly clean, at one end.

"She's overdone it, of course, in spite of all I've said to her," Jim said *sotto voce*, as he thrust open the back door. "Mabel! Are you all right?" he called, and fully expected an answer.

He didn't get one.

It did not occur to him to go into the shop first. The fact that Mabel had put the *Closed* sign in position seemed to mean that she wasn't there; the door had swung to, anyhow. An-other doorway from the small room led to the stairs, and he raced up these, elbows brushing the walls on either side, and called with increasing anxiety:

"Mabel, are you all right? *Mabel!*"

There was still no answer; and the bedroom was empty. Stone stood looking at the double bed, with the pale pink bed-spread, the matching basket-weave chair and bedside table, feeling a little stupid. She must have gone out, then; but why should she? He had never known her to close the shop before. He ought to have taken it easier; there was probably a note downstairs, explaining everything. He glanced into the small spare room, soon to be the nursery, into the bathroom and the store room where stocks of dry goods were kept; if he could get an extra $2\frac{1}{2}$ per cent discount for taking quantity, he liked to cram the goods into stock. Prices were going up, up, up all the time.

He went more slowly down the stairs, calling *"Mabel!"* half-heartedly when he entered the living-room. There was no note anywhere, and he stepped towards the shop door and opened it. As he did so, he trod on something slippery, re-gained his balance, and glanced down. He saw a red smear on the polished linoleum. It looked rather as if Mabel had upset something—probably tomato sauce. Perhaps she had an accident in the shop, stretching up to get something off a high shelf. She mustn't take risks like that.

He pulled open the door, and saw her lying between the crowded shelves and the counter.

II

SUPERINTENDENT WEST

ROGER WEST was in his office at New Scotland Yard overlooking the Embankment a little before six-thirty that evening. He was alone, his coat was off, his collar undone, his forehead shiny with sweat. The two windows were open as wide as they could be, but there was no hint of a breeze even off the Thames, which looked like a sheet of glass. Traffic noises sounded loud and urgent, as if every driver was suffering from frustration, and patience was wearing thin in unfamiliar heat.

West was signing letters. The night staff would make sure that they were taken in time to catch the night's post, and five minutes should see him away from here. He wasn't quite sure whether to look forward to the evening or not. The lawns at his Chelsea home needed cutting, his wife would try to keep him up to a promise to do them tonight, and he would try to persuade her that such exercise was too strenuous. At any other time he would have given the job to his two teenage sons, but they were away on some school camp or other, in North Wales, and wouldn't be back until Sunday.

One of the two telephones on his desk rang.

He looked at it, without enthusiasm; this could be just a formality, or could be one of the exasperating major jobs which occasionally came at this kind of awkward hour. What he would like would be some kind of a riverside inquiry, out at Richmond or Twickenham, say. He grinned, and lifted the receiver.

"West speaking."

"Mrs. West is on the line, sir."

He thought at once: "Trouble with the boys," and momentarily held his breath. Then he said: "Put her through," and told himself that he was being absurd; why shouldn't Janet ring now? But it was an odd time for her to call, for she would be expecting him home any minute. Perhaps she wanted to hurry him.

"Roger, dear," Janet greeted, and immediately his fears faded; her tone was sufficiently ingratiating to tell him that this was a request call.

"Janet, *darling*," he cooed.

Janet laughed.

"Do I sound as obvious as that?"

"Yes, dear, just as obvious as that."

"The trouble with you is that you're too clever by half," protested Janet, but she was still laughing. "Are you coming straight home?"

"Yes, but the shops are shut."

"Oh," said Janet, as if disappointed. "The thing is, dear, Mrs. Ramsden has some American cousins over from New York or New somewhere, and she's asked me to go and have a fork supper with them. It's a hen party, and——"

Roger found himself chuckling aloud.

"You go and cackle," he said. "I can find plenty to do, but I warn you that without your commanding presence the chances of the lawns getting cut are negligible."

"Oh, you needn't worry about the lawns," interrupted Janet. "I gave young Freddy Smith half a crown to cut them after school, and he's done quite a good job. Can you get a meal out, or shall I leave something?"

"I'll eat out," Roger promised. "Expensively."

"I don't mind how much you spend," said Janet. "Are you sure you won't mind?"

"Don't stay out too late," urged Roger.

Janet laughed; he laughed; and they rang off. Roger pushed his chair back after a moment's amused reflection, and went across to the window for an illusion of coolness; and as he reached it, the leaves of the plane trees on the Embankment actually rustled, and the glass-smooth surface of the water seemed as if it were ruffled, too. Three pleasure craft were coming down stream, a few small craft were being rowed; a police launch passed at slow speed. Roger poked his fingers through hair which was damp with sweat. He could drive out

to Imber Court, and have a yarn with whoever was energetic
enough to be playing tennis or cricket, he could have a swim,
or he could go to a good London restaurant and have a
trencherman's meal. The luxury of an evening completely off
was unusual; and, a little wryly, he found that he was mildly
disappointed. *How* long had he been married? Twenty odd
years, and—but he mustn't let Janet catch him saying "twenty-
odd". Nearly twenty-*three*.

He signed four more letters, pushed his chair back, and was
about to get up when the telephone rang again.

"West speaking," he answered.

"Hiyah, Handsome," said a man with a markedly Cockney
accent. "You in a good mood tonight?"

"No," said Roger promptly. "What's up?" The speaker
was Chief Superintendent Bellew, from the Clapham Division, an old Yard friend recently given the Superintendency
of the Division; Bellew was a man of his own age, whom he
both respected and liked.

"We've got a nasty one," said Bellew, "and the Big White
Chief is out."

"You tried Hardy?"

"He's gone home, too," said Bellew, and added with a mock
growl: "Comes to something when the Assistant Commissioner and the Commander C.I.D. watch the clock like
that, doesn't it? I wouldn't mind betting you're the only
senior officer on the spot, *Mr.* West."

Roger said: "What's the job, Jack?"

"A woman was attacked in her shop, late this afternoon—
less than an hour ago, I'd say. Done for, if the doc's right,"
Bellew gloomed. "The husband's nearly off his head. I'm
speaking from a telephone round the corner from the shop,
didn't want to ask if you could come with the rest of the
Metropolitan Police able to pick up the request on the air.
Looks like a cash register robbery, and the woman caught the
swine in the act. Bashed her about with some canned fruit,
or something."

After a moment's pause, Roger said: "What have you done,
so far?"

"Next to nothing, Handsome," said Bellew. "It's the kind of job where the Yard wants to get in quick, and I'd rather you were on it than anyone else. Old Dammit's with the woman now, she'll be in an ambulance in the next five minutes. Old Dammit says there isn't a chance in a thousand, too much bleeding, but she's still alive. I'm doing all the usual, but——"

"Give me the address, will you?" Roger said.

"Kemp Road, not far from Clapham Common Road," replied Bellew. "Where you used to mess around on the Raeburn job."

"Have a man waiting for me at the corner of Clapham Common Road and the High Street," said Roger. "I'll be there in about half an hour. We can square it with the Old Man in the morning."

"Thanks, Handsome." Bellew's tone was lighter. "You're a pal."

Roger said: "I don't know whether you are, yet," and rang off. He sat staring at the signed letters, the top one of which was to a North Country Police Force about a man who had "stolen" his own daughter from his estranged wife; the variety and the degrees of the crimes which passed through the hands of the Yard seemed inexhaustible. He stood up and went to the corner where he kept his "bag", a case rather like a doctor's, and which contained everything he was likely to need on an investigation. He did not have to check it, for he always kept it at the ready. He pressed a bell on his desk, and a grey-haired messenger came in.

"Post those letters for me, Joe, and tell Information I'm going over to Clapham, at Mr. Bellew's request."

"Oh, are you, sir? Give my regards to Mr. Bellew, won't you?" The messenger probably knew more senior officers of the Metropolitan Police than anyone else at the Yard. "What kind of job?"

"Could be murder."

"Well, so long as you don't forget to give my regards to Mr. Bellew," said the messenger.

Roger smiled, went out, waited for the lift, and then strode out into the sticky warmth of the evening. It was even hotter than he had realised, and heat haze rose shimmering off the macadam of the Yard. The courtyard itself had a bare and empty between six-and-seven o'clock kind of look, but several men were standing about and talking. Roger waved, then went to his own car, a black Humber. As he opened the door, he realised that he hadn't left the windows down that morning, and when he got in it was like sitting in an oven. Irritably, he opened the windows; at least movement would cool the car down a bit. A policeman at the Embankment gate waved him on, and he swung right, towards Westminster Bridge; the traffic on the far side would be thinner than here, and in any case he had missed the thickest of the rush hour hold-ups. Big Ben was striking the quarter past six as he turned left at the filter-light, and on to the bridge.

He kept thinking of a woman being battered with a tin of fruit; somehow, that made the affair hideous. And he kept reminding himself that the assailant was somewhere among London's sweating eight millions: one man with a heavy weight on his conscience.

Or a man without a conscience.

He wished he were going home to cut those lawns.

. . . . .

Ringed round with white chalk circles on the floor of the shop, near the doorway leading to the back of the shop, were three tins of Golden Syrup. The lid of one of these had come off when it had been used as a weapon, and the thick syrup had oozed out, so that it spread over an area nearly too wide for a man to step across; at one patch, blood was mixed with it. Other chalked white lines surrounded patches of blood, and someone had shown sense and initiative by tapping some nails into the blue linoleum, and twisting white cotton round each one to make an outline of the woman's body; there was too much syrup and blood for chalk marks. One spot had been marked with a loop of string, and inside it was a piece of a finger-nail; the nail must have been too long, and it was dirty.

Bellew, a very big man who looked like the popular idea of

a sailor, was standing against the counter. His double-breasted navy blue suit was a little too tight for him, and shiny at the seat and across the shoulders. Roger was looking at some notes that Bellew had made; notes of things he had already started to do. One was a door-to-door call on every house in Kemp Road and the turnings off, to find out if anyone had seen the man who had done this dreadful thing. Another note said that James Stone, the husband, had gone to the hospital with his wife. The police surgeon had gone to the hospital, too.

Outside, Roger knew, a hundred or so people had been attracted by the news, the ambulances and the rumours. He had seen at least a dozen youths on cycles, several motor-cyclists, and more than twenty people walking towards the corner shop. The Press would be here before long, if it wasn't already represented.

He went to the till. The drawer was open, and a few pieces of small silver as well as a section full of pennies, halfpennies and threepenny pieces were on view. Some chalk marks were on the handle, too, and on the front of the drawer.

"Could be fingerprints there," Bellew said. "Thought we'd better make sure."

"Yes. Could be. Any children?"

"One on the way."

"None at school?"

"Childless couple," Bellew said.

"How many men have you out checking?"

"Twenty-four. Fairly quiet afternoon for my chaps, and I slapped 'em all on to overtime. Got a few grumbles until they knew what it was about."

"Daresay you did," said Roger. He looked and felt very bleak. "Anyone any idea how much cash there was in the till?"

"No, but most Thursday nights they have about forty quid. I saw that in the paying-in book of the bank, for Fridays."

"All this, for forty pounds," Roger said heavily. "It doesn't seem to make sense. Any other man in the woman's life?"

"Dunno yet, but judging from a neighbour, they were very happy about a kid being on the way."

"Hm. Better check as usual, though—it might not be just what it seems to be." Roger stretched out his hand and picked up one of the tins of Golden Syrup. "Always did think these weighed heavy," he remarked. "Jack, this is a job for Appleby, if I can get him. Anyone used that telephone?"

"It had some of the woman's dabs on, that's all."

"Thanks," said Roger. He lifted the receiver and dialled a St. John's Wood number. From outside, a man said: "Keep back, please." It was very warm in the shop, and there was no cross breeze, no hint of coolness. As he listened to the ringing sound, Roger looked at the big man with him, and the half-dozen other men who were taking photographs, searching for finger and footprints, going through all the routine of the early stages of an investigation. Bellew had directed them well; no one would touch anything that even looked like a clue.

"Jack, I've been thinking," Roger began, and then the ringing sound broke off, and a woman announced:

"This is Dr. Appleby's house."

"Is Dr. Appleby in, please?" As Roger asked his tone changed, reminding him immediately of Janet's; like her he wanted to make a good impression.

"He is, but he's in the bath," the woman said, irritably. "Who is that?"

"Superintendent West speaking, ma'am."

"Oh, *damn*!" the woman said, vexedly. "You don't want to drag him out tonight, do you?"

"I think he ought to know about this case," Roger said. "I'm really sorry."

After a pause, the woman said: "Well, I'll see if he can come," and with ill grace she banged down the receiver. Roger grimaced. Bellew shrugged, and eased his collar, and the policeman outside raised his voice to the crowd: "*Get back, I tell you.*"

"Jack," said Roger, very thoughtfully, "how many shop robberies have you had recently?"

"Half a dozen or so this month, I suppose," Bellew answered at once. "What's on your mind?"

"Just a thought," said Roger. "How many with violence?"

"One here and there," said Bellew, "but none so vicious as this."

"That's as well."

"Shop raids come in waves," said Bellew. "You know that as well as I do."

"Yes," agreed Roger. "See those shelves packed with cigarettes?"

Bellew swivelled round. The narrow shelves with a few cigarettes were near the cash register, easy for handing to a customer at the till. There were a dozen different brands, but only a few packets of each; two of the piles had obviously been disturbed.

"Better find out what kind of stock of cigarettes they carried, and whether any stocks were taken," Roger said. "A regular customer should know. I—oh, hallo, Doc." He heard Dr. Dan Appleby's voice, with its familiar: "*Now what's all this about?*" and he gave Appleby time to grumble before he went on:

"I'd very much like you to come over to Kemp Road, Clapham, where there's been a shop robbery, a woman badly injured and probably dying, and a lot of blood."

"Be right over," answered Appleby.

"Dan!" came a protesting voice further away from the telephone.

"Thanks very much," said Roger. He rang off, pleased, and immediately heard a woman's voice raised, outside in the street. He was thinking so much about Dan Appleby and his home problem, and about the idea which had struck him about other shop robberies, that he didn't pay the woman much attention. Then suddenly her words pierced the protecting veil of thought.

"I tell you I must go inside and see my son."

Bellew said: "Oh, Gawd," and Roger's mind was jolted off everything except the fact that the woman outside was the stricken husband's mother. And he would have to see her.

III

APPLEBY

ROGER nodded to Bellew, who walked across to the door, careful to avoid treading where there were any marks. He reached it as a policeman tapped. Bellew opened the door, and Roger caught sight of a small, well-preserved woman, dressed in a tailored suit of pale green, a big policeman behind her, a crowd of fifty or sixty people pressing close, and a tall newspaperman whom he recognised as from the *Daily Echo*. The policeman looked hot and flustered. Another man, out of sight, said exasperatedly: "*Keep back, please.*"

Bellew stood aside for the neatly dressed woman to enter. She looked surprisingly cool, although her forehead was damp, and so was the grey hair which grew in a pronounced widow's peak. Bellew stepped outside, obviously to give his men instructions, perhaps partly to leave this difficult moment to Roger.

The woman hardly came up to Roger's shoulder. She had clear, very pale blue eyes and small features. She was well-dressed and neatly made-up. He judged her to be in the middle fifties.

"I'm very sorry about this," Roger said. "I'm Chief Detective Superintendent West, of New Scotland Yard." By saying that slowly, he always managed to gain a few seconds, and it seemed to make what he had to say more significant. "Do I understand that you are Mr. Stone's mother?"

"I am," she said. "Where is he?"

"He's gone to the hospital, with your daughter-in-law," Roger answered, gently. "I'm afraid that she's very badly hurt."

Mrs. Stone said: "Oh." It was hard to judge what she felt, possible only to see that she was giving herself time to get used to this situation. Roger wondered how much she had heard, how distorted rumour had been. "Oh," she said, again, and for a moment closed her eyes. "She isn't——" she broke off.

"Her injuries haven't yet proved fatal," Roger said, still gently. He looked round and pulled up a stool, and held it in position. "Won't you sit down?"

She ignored the invitation as she went on sharply:

"How bad is she?"

"Very badly injured, I'm afraid."

"Is my—is my son all right?"

"Perfectly, except for the shock."

"Oh," she said. "Yes, of course. Shock. Can I—can I go to the hospital at once, please? May I phone for a taxi?" She glanced at the telephone. "I must go and see my son."

"I'll put a car at your disposal," Roger promised. "Will you give us a little help before you go?" When she stood without answering, he went on: "How did you come to hear of this, Mrs. Stone?"

"A friend from across the road, a Mrs. Jackson, telephoned and told me something had happened, there was an ambulance outside here." She bit her lips. "Are you sure my son isn't hurt?"

"Quite sure, Mrs. Stone. He wasn't here when it happened."

"When *what* happened?" she demanded, and suddenly her voice rose. "Why doesn't someone tell me what happened to my daughter-in-law?"

. . . . .

Roger told the story briskly. The news seemed to quieten, even to numb her. Roger sent her to the hospital in one of the Divisional cars, and spent ten more minutes with Bellew, who had brought uniformed reinforcements to control the crowd, and was much happier. Reports from several neighbours made it clear that Stone had been out on his delivery, and one old woman, a Mrs. Klein, had said that she had seen Mabel at 5.15, at her living-room window; another had said that Stone had returned just before half past five. At least they had narrowed down the time of the attack.

"The mother's a cut above the daughter-in-law," Bellew

remarked. "Wonder if any of my chaps know anything about her."

"Will you find out and let me know?" asked Roger.

Then Dan Appleby arrived.

Roger could remember the time when he, as the youngest Chief Inspector at the Yard, had nevertheless been old enough to feel some resentment towards the pathologist when Appleby had first been appointed by the Home Office. Then—as now— he had seemed to be little more than a boy. No one knew how he did it, but he always managed to look as if a shave once a week was all he needed. He had very fair, downy hair, and darker eyebrows and lashes, which gave him a startled, in- genuous appearance, as if he were constantly in a state of sur- prise. To make the general impression worse, he stammered slightly, especially when thinking ahead. It had seemed im- possible that a lad fresh from medical school could possibly be of service to experienced detectives who were twice and some even thrice his age. But after five years, every Yard man who was in a hurry tried to get Appleby. He had an astounding faculty of observation and of interpreting what he observed.

Appleby entered the shop, blinking a little, upper lip beaded with sweat, making the sparse hairs look slightly dirty. He carried a black bag rather like Roger's; he wore a biscuit coloured linen coat and a pair of thick flannel trousers. He looked round the shop, then up at the ceiling, then at the door and the floor, before he glanced at Roger and said:

"My w-w-w-wife hates you."

"Well," Roger said, "I didn't marry her."

"That's a p-p-p-point," said Appleby. "Keeping c-c-cool?" He didn't offer to shake hands, but squatted on his haunches, and studied the chalk marks and the blood. Then he stood up and studied the treacle tins. "She dead or alive?"

"The reports aren't very hopeful."

"After this lot, they wouldn't be," Appleby declared. "The man must have gone mad. I'll go and have a look at her, but I don't mind admitting that there isn't much I can tell you from this. Not much that you don't know, anyhow. She was com- ing out of the back room, probably trying to take the man by

surprise—just about here, I should say." Appleby moved to
the right, stepping clear of the glutinous pool of syrup. "See?"

Roger saw a few splashes of syrup, still oozing slowly down-
wards, on the door jamb; he also saw several little globules of
the gooey stuff on some packets of soap powder and detergents.

"No, I don't see," he said.

"The chap was at the till, obviously," declared Appleby.
"That's where she would surprise him. You can see where he
turned round, see where the golden syrup is on display—he
must have been within hands' reach of those. He threw one,
that's when he caught his finger-nail in the ridge round the
lid. The tin caught the woman in the face, ricocheted off,
banged into the shelf here—see the mark?—and that's what
forced the lid off. Those treacle tin lids are stuck on pretty
tight, they need a lot of levering, or else a sharp knock. So this
was a glancing blow. The lid came off, the syrup sprayed the
soaps and things and the door, then fell where it is now."

As he talked, Appleby kept pointing; to marks on the floor
and on the wall, and to the different packets of goods. Roger
was aware of a strange atmosphere in the shop. One after
another, Bellew's men stopped what they were doing, and
watched the pathologist. Now Appleby's stammer had quite
gone, and his clear-cut assertions seemed to be borne out by
all the evidence available. When he stopped, there was silence.
He glanced at Bellew, gave a brief smile, and said:

"W-w-w-what have I g-g-g-got wrong, Superintendent."

"I'll tell you when I've had time to work it out," said Bellew, heavily. "What about the next tin?"

"The w-w-w-what? Oh, the second tin. He used that as a
hammer." Appleby pointed to a tin at the side of the counter.
"Couldn't be any other explanation. Blood all round the
bottom rim. Used the bottom of it, probably a tin turned up-
side down when he grabbed the first one and knocked the pile
over. You can see hairs, skin and even bone fragments on the
bottom rim. Shouldn't think he was all that powerful a man—
no need to keep hitting her as he did, if he were. Got any
fingerprints?"

"We think so," Bellew said.

"Fat lot of use thinking so," grumbled Appleby. "Well, I-I-I-I'll trot along to the hospital, look her over, and then get back home." He smiled at Roger. "M-m-m-my wife would hate anybody who took me away from home on our wedding anniversary. In b-b-bad enough already, I forgot it until I was reminded. You'll ph-ph-phone me at home, after nine-thirty, say. Right?"

"Yes, Doc," Roger said, humbly.

"Or come and s-s-s-see me," suggested Appleby, with a broad grin. "That m-m-might get me in good. Any woman would b-b-be happy to see a fine, handsome, upstanding young chap like you"

They all laughed.

"He takes the biscuit," Bellew remarked, when Appleby had left. "One look, and he tells you exactly what happened. Think he's right?"

"I've only known him wrong once," Roger said, "and I've often done my damnedest to trip him up. He was fooled when a hit and run driver was at the wheel of a car with a left hand drive. Now, what we want are those prints." He went to the till, and studied the grey fingerprint powder marks on it; these showed up as the faint outlines of several fingers. He opened his own case, took out his magnifying glass, and bent down over the three tins; they were sticky with syrup tinged with blood, and the syrup had almost certainly oozed in such a way that all the prints had been blurred out of recognition. "We want just one clear one," he said. "One thing's certain—he didn't wear gloves."

"Sounds to me like one of those bloody amateurs," said Bellew.

"Look here," said Roger, "this tin's fairly clean on the underside. If we pick it up with a pair of calipers, we might be able to get photographs of any prints underneath. Who's your man?"

"Pardy!" called Bellew, to one of his men. "Bring your bag of tricks over here."

Ten minutes later, they had a good photograph of three prints, two of which coincided with smears found on the till and with a faint print found on a one pound note which had lodged in a basket of special-offer sardines near the door. Everything they discovered seemed to bear out Dan Appleby's theory, and the presence of the little pathologist was still felt when, an hour afterwards, the police had photographed everything they wanted.

By then, it was eight o'clock. Roger was hungry, and the heat was still sticky; now that he was able to relax, he felt it close about him. He lit a cigarette from Bellew's lighter, and as he did so, a policeman appeared at the doorway.

"Message for you, Mr. West."

"What is it?"

"It's from the hospital, sir."

"How is she?"

"She's gone," the policeman announced, and immediately there was a gasp from the crowd outside, an oath from an unseen man, and tightening lips among the policemen still on duty.

"The husband's on his way to his mother's place," the policeman went on. "That's 17, River View Crescent, Lambeth, Mr. West—on this side of the river, between Battersea and Lambeth."

"So we'll soon find out all there is to know about Mrs. S. senior," Bellew said. "Runs a hostel of sorts, I'm told."

"Of sorts?"

"Big place, rather like a Youth Hostel—place where business people can get reasonably priced rooms and cheap food," explained Bellew. "It's made up of several converted houses."

In fact River View Hostel occupied most of a crescent of four storey houses, a little way from the Thames, but with nothing between it and the Embankment, so that all the front and most of the side rooms had a view of the river. The old-fashioned, Victorian facade of weathered red brick led Roger to expect high ceilings, big doors, a curiously depressing gloom of staircases and passages, but everything had been recently decorated, and the place was obviously well-maintained. There was certainly nothing gloomy or depressing about the big room on the fourth floor where Mrs. Stone was with her son. It was beautifully appointed, and somehow unexpectedly opulent here, although it suited this petite, well-dressed, well-groomed woman.

On the way over, one of Bellew's men had told Roger that Mrs. Stone was the manager of the hostel, which had nearly a hundred rooms, many of which were occupied by business men and women; and half of them had kitchens.

"Lot of Cockells Stores' managers live there," the man had said.

Jim Stone was standing by the window, looking over the river, when Roger went in; and he seemed hardly aware of Roger's presence.

"I've got to avenge her," he said in a hard voice. "I won't be able to rest until I've killed the devil."

"Jim, it's no use talking like that," Mrs. Stone protested, with forced calm. "It won't help to bring Mabel back. Will it, Inspector?"

"I tell you I've got to avenge her."

"Mr. Stone," Roger said, very quietly, "there is a way in which you can help. The law will punish the man once we've caught him—and from what you've told me, you might be able to help to identify him positively. I need the clearest possible description of anyone you saw leaving the street, and it must be accurate in every detail."

"But how can you be sure——?" began the small woman.

Roger motioned her to silence. She opened her mouth again as if to protest, then moved back, obviously acknowledging that he might be talking sense. Stone was staring into Roger's eyes, and Roger had never seen greater pain in a man's face, or deeper anguish in a man's eyes.

Stone was in the late twenties or early thirties. He was tall, broad-shouldered, good-looking in a rather odd way—his nose was a little on one side, his eyes were deep set and the sockets seemed to be chiselled, adding to the look of anguish. The square chin had a pronounced cleft, often an illusory guide to character. Unexpectedly his voice was public school, unusual for a back street grocer.

"There was a man. I only just saw him when he looked

round," he said. "He was small, and he had a pointed nose, that's all I'm sure of. But—I'll never forget him."

"Describing the face of a man you saw fifty yards away isn't always easy," Roger said, "but if you can tell us what clothes he was wearing, what kind of figure he had, whether you noticed any peculiarity about his walk—anything of that kind can help us to find others who might have seen him when he reached the High Street. We had two policemen on duty about that time, near the cinema—one of them might be able to pick up the description and help us to trace the man. Don't make any mistake, there's a great deal that you can do to help us find him, and if he's the man . . ."

"You won't hang him," Stone said, flatly. "Not these days."

"Murder in the course of robbery is a capital charge," Roger reminded him.

"They're all fools," Stone said. "They'll let him off. I'd like to deal with him myself."

"You can't, Mr. Stone," Roger said, "unless you already have some idea who it is."

Stone stared, as if uncomprehending, then looked startled. His mother moved forward.

"What was that remark supposed to mean?" she demanded.

"Has Mr. Stone any enemies? Had Mrs. Stone——?"

"I've told you already, no, she hadn't," said Stone, slowly. "There was no reason in the world why anyone should hurt Mabel. She was the kindest person alive." His voice didn't break, but Roger saw the woman turn away, as if to hide her feelings. "And the man who killed her has got to die, too. I'm going to find him, and I'm going to kill him."

"Jim, don't talk like that," said his mother huskily.

"I'm going to find him, and I'm going to kill him, if it takes me the rest of my life," Stone declared. "It isn't any use trying to fool me," he went on to Roger. "It's no use talking to me about the law. *I'm* going to find him."

"Inspector——" the woman began.

"In your son's position I would feel exactly the same," Roger said. "And after what we've seen, there's hardly a man on the Force who wouldn't like to choke the life out of this killer. Mr. Stone, I must be on my way. If there's anything at all I can do, please telephone me."

He turned to the door of an apartment with one long, lovely room overlooking the river. There was still sufficient light to show the couples walking, and old men strolling, and dogs lolloping and youths skylarking. Roger left Stone standing erect and silent, while Stone's mother came hurrying after him.

"Inspector, what shall I do with him?" she asked. "I've never known him like this. He means it, can't you see that? He means what he says."

"If we argue with him now it will only make him stubborn," Roger said. "We need your help too, Mrs. Stone. He won't tell me but he may tell you exactly what this man looked like. I'll see you tomorrow morning. Meanwhile if I were you I wouldn't argue too much, I'd just go along with him. That can't do any harm," Roger went on, reassuringly. "He'll never find the man by himself; the talk is just a safety valve."

"I hope you're right," the woman said. "When do you think the shop can be opened again?"

"We should be through by the morning," Roger said. The question jarred, and yet was understandable, especially when Stone's mother went on:

"My son will be better when he's got something to do. I think it would drive him mad if he hung about here doing nothing. He——" she broke off. "Help him all you can, Inspector, won't you?"

"In every way we can," Roger promised. "I'm going straight to Scotland Yard now, in the hope of getting some news."

IV

ROBBERIES BY THE DOZEN

THERE was no news about the Stone murder at the Yard, but there was a pencilled message on Roger's desk: "*Dr. Appleby rang, and said what about it?*" There was also a fairly lengthy message from Bellew. Roger read this, and looked at his watch; it was half past ten. He smiled wryly, and went down to his car. He was still hungry, although he had had a sandwich and a coffee at the Clapham Police Station

Instead of going home, he headed for the St. John's Wood area, and within fifteen minutes he was turning into the front garden of the house where Dan Appleby had a flat. Roger had never been here, but had passed by when driving with the pathologist; Appleby had pointed to the window several times, so Roger knew that it was on the third floor at the front.

Lights shone at several windows.

He went into the fairly modern house, found the hallway well-decorated and newly painted, and an automatic lift waiting. The lighting was bright. The board announced: "*Dr. D. F. Appleby, M.D., Apartment 5.*" The lift moved even more slowly than the one at the Yard, yet stopped with a jolt. The black-painted door of No. 5 was immediately opposite. Roger pressed the bell, and heard it ring some distance inside the flat.

There was no immediate response, and he began to wonder whether the blaze of lights had fooled him; he had assumed from it that no intimate celebration of the anniversary was pre-occupying the Applebys. He was about to ring again when footsteps sounded. Appleby opened the door, wearing only a short-sleeved shirt and a pair of pale-coloured slacks. His hair was slightly dishevelled.

"M-my w-w-w-wife hates you even more," he said. "C-c-come on in."

Roger followed him in.

"T-t-t-ten minutes later and we'd have gone to bed," said Appleby. "That room on the right." He thrust the door wide open, and Roger stepped into a room rather like Mrs. Stone's, but furnished in more modern fashion, and quite beautifully appointed. Standing near the fireplace was a woman, half a head taller than Appleby. She wore a close-fitting house-coat of sapphire blue, high at the neck, with long sleeves. The light fell in such a way that her features showed up vividly; she was exceptionally good-looking. Dark as her husband was fair, she had deep blue eyes, a clear complexion and the kind of figure which seemed to promise even when it was in repose. Roger was so taken aback that he almost gaped.

"H-here's the big blonde beast," Dan Appleby said. "Roger West, placate my wife for me. She hasn't forgiven me for being out most of the evening." He gave his wife a charming smile. "Dot, this is the man you keep reading about, Handsome West of the Yard."

Mrs. Appleby held out her hand, and said: "I don't know what is worse, having to live with him or having to work with him." Her hand was warm but dry. Her gaze was frank and appraising. At first sight it was impossible to imagine what she had seen in Dan Appleby to marry him.

"Living with him, I'm sure," Roger said. "After all, I can resign."

Appleby laughed. "That'll be the day. Had any dinner?"

"Yes, thanks, I——"

"Man's a liar," Appleby said to his wife. "I telephoned Bellew, who said the most he'd had was a boiled beef sandwich. Think you could rustle up some of that salmon, Dot?"

"No, really——" Roger began.

Mrs. Appleby laughed. "Don't give it a thought. I have to feed my husband whenever he's got time to put on a bib. I won't be five minutes." She moved towards the door, and Roger found himself almost hypnotised, watching her until she went out and the door closed.

"Ah-hem, don't they say?" said Appleby.

Roger grinned, colouring slightly.

"And the marvel is, she puts up with me," went on Appleby. "What will you have? We've nearly everything."

"A whisky and soda would be just right."

"I shall have gin," said Appleby. "Don't know what I like about the damned stuff, but I do. N-n-now, Handsome." He went towards a small flat-topped cabinet where a dozen bottles and some glasses were on show. "I don't think I've anything to add to what I said in the shop. No doubt that second treacle tin was used as a hammer. You can tell the husband that the first or at worst the second blow knocked Mrs. Stone unconscious. No need to say there was a miscarriage. What's he like?"

"Full of vengeance," Roger said, and took a glass which had plenty of whisky in it; Appleby squirted in a splash of soda. "Fill it up, will you?" He waited. "And at the moment he means it."

"Any idea who the killer was?"

"We've some prints but they aren't in Records," said Roger. "I'd hoped we'd have some luck."

"Amateur, then?"

Roger said: "Well, it almost looks like it. No gloves, and he left a lot of prints behind, but even an old lag can get careless. Thing is, he needn't have killed her if he'd worn a mask or a scarf over his face. The fact that he killed suggests that she would have recognised him again."

"Friend of the family, do you mean?"

"I don't yet know what I mean," Roger said.

Appleby sipped his drink; Roger drank half of his at one go.

"What's on your mind?" Appleby asked.

"Shop robberies," answered Roger, heavily. "Bellew checked tonight, and left a message at the Yard. He remembered a half-dozen, but in fact they've had eleven in the Clapham area in the past three months. I picked up some figures at the Yard, too. There have been at least a hundred similar robberies in the past three months in the Metropolitan area, and I daresay that when we've added them all up, it will come to nearer two hundred."

"How many with violence?"

Roger said: "That's what worries me."

"Worries me, too," said Appleby. "How many?"

"I know of twelve, but nothing like this case. Usually the thieves wore masks, to make sure they weren't recognised. That's what makes this one different—as if the chap didn't care if he was recognised or not."

"Meaning he came prepared to kill? With a treacle tin?"

"You don't need to carry a weapon," Roger said. "If you came to kill, you could use your hands or anything handy."

"Couldn't be overdoing this angle, could you?" inquired Appleby mildly.

"Oh, I could be," Roger admitted. "As Bellew pointed out, these shop raids often come in waves. But there have been a hell of a lot, and there's obviously a possibility of big scale organisation."

"Could be, I daresay," conceded Appleby. "So you're worried about shop crimes in general, and this one is particularly puzzling."

"That's it."

Appleby said: "How many robberies are known to have been by the same man?"

"I talked to several witnesses, and the description in each case was different," Roger said. "The differences were much more than the usual variation in description because of differing powers of observation. Different men were almost certainly involved."

"And when you check in the morning, you may find that this one is different, too," observed Appleby. "Any common factor at all?"

"Yes."

"Don't h-h-hold out on me."

"Whenever violence was done, something found in the raided shop was used as a weapon," Roger said. "More often than not it was a bottle—such as a bottle of orange squash. A tin or a can was used on two jobs. Twice——" He broke off, for his memory was ticking over very fast, while he was recalling the circumstances of cases which he had not himself handled. "Twice a bacon knife was used. The weapon was always left in the shop, too."

"Handsome, I can see you're worried," said Appleby, "but who would organise small-time robberies like that?" When Roger made no comment, Appleby went on: "Do you know how much was stolen tonight?"

"Just under fifty pounds in cash, and about a hundred pounds' worth of cigarettes and chocolates. Bellew got the figures for me. There's a girl assistant at the shop, who goes to technical college on Thursday afternoons. She was able to say what the stocks had been this morning, so we know that the total taken was a hundred and fifty poundsworth, at the most."

"Do that often enough, and it spells money," remarked Appleby.

"But with an organisation there are a lot of people to share it with," Roger pointed out. He was whirling the whisky and soda round in his glass as he went on: "I know what you mean, though. If these raids are organised by a receiver who pays cash for the stolen goods, say, he would get the goods for next to nothing, and the thief would keep the cash. One receiver could have ten or a dozen or twenty people doing the jobs, too, but——"

Appleby broke in: "Can anyone employ a dozen or twenty raiders all prepared to kill?"

Roger didn't answer, and before Appleby could make any other comment, footsteps sounded at the door, and he stepped across to open it. His wife came in carrying a tray with lettuce, tomato, the pink succulence of a piece of fresh salmon, brown bread, biscuits, butter and cheese.

"Don't I get fed too?" demanded Appleby.

"If you eat anything else tonight, I'll leave you," said Dorothy Appleby. "You're getting disgustingly fat. Now if you had a figure like Mr. West, you could eat as much as you liked. Tea, coffee or beer, Mr. West?"

V

BODY

NEARLY a week later, on the Thursday morning, Roger made a dash for the front of his garage, where his younger son, Richard, was pushing open the door against the whiplike fury of a gale-force wind. Low clouds scudded, sometimes almost as low as the rooftops in this pleasant Chelsea street. Trees which had been fresh looking and picture-pretty a week before were bowed down by a wind which howled and whined and carried bucketsful of rain, splashing and hissing. A corner of Roger's lawn was under inches of rippling water. Beds of antirrhinums, asters, delphiniums and geraniums were waving about as if in desperate panic.

"Coo, what a morning," Richard exclaimed. "Think it's safe to drive, Dad?"

"I'll manage," Roger said, dryly. "Put that mac over your head and run for it. You'll have to leave ten minutes earlier for school this morning."

"Be a jolly good excuse for being late," Richard said, and added a little wistfully: "We're hardly ever late." He gave a bright grin, hitched the mackintosh up, and said: "'Bye, Dad. Catch lots of crooks!" and made a dive for the open front door. Janet was there, to wave, then to look gloomily on the wreckage of the garden.

Near the corner of Bell Street some slates had been blown off a roof; at the corner the whiplash fury of the wind caught a struggling cyclist and made him get off his machine. Three cars were crawling along, not daring to pass. Roger fell into line. It was nearly half past eight, and he was due at the Yard at nine o'clock for some special briefing on a jewellery smash-and-grab job which had set the Yard by the ears and the Press by the headline the previous day. This morning's newspapers hadn't yet arrived; when they did, the smash-and-grab job would have priority. By bad luck it had taken place within a

37

stone's throw of Savile Row Police Station; there would be
some raucous Press comments about it.

Roger felt virtually sure of one thing; this would prise him
off the investigation into Mabel Stone's murder, and he didn't
know whether to be pleased or sorry. He had made very little
progress, although he had concentrated on the inquiry and
touched practically nothing else. He had interviewed hundreds of people who had seen or might have seen the murderer,
but there was still no real clue to his identity.

Almost certainly because Mrs. Stone had been expecting the
child, the newspapers had given the murder and the subse-
quent hunt much more space than most shop robberies—more,
in fact, than Roger could remember on any of them; usually
there was nothing spectacular or really sensational about that
kind of sordid crime. But he could not complain of the support
the Press had given him. An *Echo* artist had drawn a com-
posite picture of the man seen to leave the shop, gleaned from
many neighbours' accounts, and the picture had taken up a lot
of the front page not only of the *Echo* but of the *Sunday Globe*,
with its six million circulation.

Reports, all valueless, had come in from all over London.
Bellew as well as a section of the Yard had spent the whole
week sifting through these, and while no one had yet said so,
Roger expected to be taken off the job this morning. It would
become a simple matter of routine, and he would be reas-
signed later if anything new came in.

If he had a complaint, it was that none of his superiors had
been impressed by his "organised shop robbery" theory.
Closer inspection of all the records had shown a lot of differences among the crimes, and the variations in the descriptions
of the thieves had been very wide.

"Shouldn't waste much time on that angle," the Commander of the Criminal Investigation Department had said,
and that had been tantamount to an order.

One of the unexpected things to develop had been a growth
of liking for Jim Stone. One met murderers, witnesses, victims, and the relatives of victims, and they passed before one
rather like pictures on a screen, real and vivid enough at the

moment of contact, but soon half forgotten. Stone made a deep impression, partly because of his cold and deliberate persistence in saying that he meant to find the murderer, and kill him; partly because there was something clean cut and likeable about him. In a way, and although he was twice Martin's age, Stone reminded Roger of his own older son.

A pleasant but ugly girl named Gwen Fowey was looking after the shop, with temporary help.

After the day of the funeral, Monday, Stone himself had made the local deliveries, but he had coupled this with questions to neighbours, nearby shop keepers, and others he knew, about the appearance of the killer. He did all this with a single-minded application which suggested that whatever the cost he meant to track down the man. Roger began to wonder whether the highly improbable would happen, whether Stone would find a clue to the killer's identity. If he did, he certainly wouldn't come to the police.

The situation could become delicate and difficult.

Roger slowed down to turn into the Yard as rain in huge drops scudded across it. He had seldom seen the courtyard so empty, and all the spaces near the doors were filled. He had a struggle to get the car door open, then staggered across to the main entrance, went up the long flight of stone steps, and paused at the top to get his breath back and to shake the rain off his trilby and his raincoat.

"Talk about flaming June," complained the sergeant on duty at the top of the steps. "Just about the worst basinful we've had for years, sir, ain't it?"

"Remember we had summer last week," Roger said mechanically, and went up with four others in the lift, then along to his office, which was quite small, but had that river view. The Chief Inspector who normally worked with him was on holiday, and he was managing with temporary and spasmodic help. On his desk was the usual pile of reports, a big fat folder of the Stone case, and pinned to it a pencilled note:

"*Please telephone Mr. Bellew.*"

Roger picked up a telephone at once, for the Stone case was

still on top of his mind. Two Chief Inspectors looked in, but
didn't stay. Roger nodded to them, then saw another note on
his desk:

"Commander's Conference postponed to 10.30."

"Get me Clapham—Mr. Bellew," Roger said, and held on.
Bellew was an early bird, and his day seldom started later than
eight o'clock. Roger sat on the corner of his brown pedestal
desk, swinging one leg, looking out of the window and just
able to see the wind whipping the Thames into foot high
waves. Clouds actually misted the top of the County Hall.

Bellew said: "That you, Handsome?"

"What's on, Jack?"

"We've got a body I want you and young Stone to see. Can
you come right over?"

The obvious answer was "No" in view of the morning's
conference. Roger hesitated.

"Yes," he said at last. "If you swear that it's vitally urgent."

"It's vitally urgent," Bellew declared. "Come straight to my
office, will you? The body's in our morgue."

.   .   .   .   .

Roger watched the morgue attendant as he switched on the
light over the top of a stone slab where a body lay covered by
a sheet of green canvas. The man, elderly and plump and
rubicund, seemed to take a delight in what he was doing, pulling down a corner of the sheet with almost loving care. As
Roger watched, he realised that this was deliberate; Bellew had
laid it on. Bellew was standing by his, Roger's side, with
an unmistakable air of expectancy. At first this was puzzling,
for the corpse's short hair was between colours, the forehead smoothed in death to an alabaster-like pallor, and all
seemed ordinary enough. Then the face took on a different
meaning—it was virtually the face of the *Echo* artist's drawing. When the sheet was down and folded beneath the chin,
the chin itself showed sharper and more pointed, but that was
the main difference.

"How did he die?" asked Roger.

Bellew said: "Turn him over, Sergeant."

"Take it easy," Roger said. "Appleby ought to have a look at him."

"Don't want Appleby for this," said Bellew. He helped the attendant to turn the body over, and to show the half-dozen or more stab wounds in the back. Roger, used to such sights, frowned at this one.

"Now I've got a bit of news for you," went on Bellew. "There were some tacky spots on the coat, trousers and on one shoe. I did a quick test. It was syrup."

Roger said: "Well, well."

"And if you doubt who this chap is, look," said Bellew, and lifted a flaccid hand. "See the torn nail of the right fore-finger? He killed Mabel Stone all right. The picture was so good that this chap was bound to be found sooner or later. Think he was killed to stop him from talking?"

"Could be," Roger said, cautiously. He was wondering what his superiors would say if he worried them on that theory again. "Do you know who he is?"

"Nothing in his pockets, but there was a find in his trousers pocket, a cleaning mark they overlooked," answered Bellew. "We'll trace him all right, and you've got another murder investigation on your hands. The big boys can't take you off it now, even if they are annoyed by the smash-and-grab job."

"You'd be surprised," said Roger.

Later that day however, he was told to concentrate on the stabbing murder.

By the evening all newspapers carried a photograph of the dead man, and copies of the photograph were at all London and Home Counties Police Stations. A team of Yard and Divisional men worked through the dry cleaners of the East End of London, and in the middle of the following afternoon, just a week after the murder of Mrs. Stone, the manager of a small firm with five branches identified not only the tag, but also the dead man. He was Lionel Endicott, he lived at Brasher's Row, Whitechapel, he was married to a girl much younger than himself—a girl in her early twenties, whereas Endicott, according to the information, was in his middle forties. That squared with the medical estimate.

Just before five o'clock on that same afternoon, Roger turned into Brasher's Row's narrow gloom, saw the terraces of little houses on either side, the unending drabness, and the children playing in the wet streets, for the storm had died down during the night although it had only just stopped raining.

It was sticky and warm, many front doors and windows were open, but the door and the window of Number 37, where Endicott had lived, was tightly closed. Roger pulled up just opposite this door, and a dozen kids ran towards him. Almost as soon as he stopped several more windows went up, and more women and men appeared at doorways. Roger was quite sure that word of his progress had preceded him in every street in this neighbourhood, and the people had simply wondered where he was going to call. He got out, and the Divisional Detective Sergeant with him followed, from the other side of the car.

Roger glanced up, saw a curtain move, and saw a woman's face at the window. He could not mistake the fear in her eyes.

VI

FEAR

RUTH ENDICOTT had been frightened since half past eight that morning, although at first the fear had been vague and shadowy. During the day, it had grown to gigantic proportions, to a state of terror, and although this had subsided, it flared up again when she saw the black car slide to a standstill outside her tiny house.

The first realisation that something was wrong had come on waking. She had been alone in bed. At night, she often was. She had learned to expect Lionel to come in late, often in the early hours of the morning, just as she had learned to expect a lot of other things: Lionel's violent outbursts of temper, his cruelty whenever she annoyed him, cruelty so different from his demanding amiability when he was in a good mood. Looking back, she still couldn't understand why she had married him, except for his money. It had really been a combination of circumstances, including being sick to death of living in a small back room, all that she could afford, and sick to death of being pestered by men because she lived alone. She had been overjoyed that one of them thought enough of her to offer marriage.

The odd thing was that Lionel had given her everything he had promised. The little house was well-furnished and newly decorated, they had a 21-inch television set, a record player, a washing-machine, a fridge—everything a housewife could want—and in that way at least she was the envy of her neighbours.

But on the whole, apart from those occasions when he lost his temper and seemed to go crazy, life wasn't so bad. She could never understand his wild outbursts, but had a vague kind of impression that he was taking something out on her—that someone else was kicking him, and he had a temperament which made him want to hurt someone in return. Only twice had he marked her permanently: once when he had struck her on the ear with a heavy mug, so that the ear lobe had split; and once when he had smashed a dinner plate on her hand. She still had a scar on the back of that hand, red and unsightly.

She did not know for certain what Lionel did for a living, and he never talked about it. Once, when she had asked him, he had flown into one of those wild rages; that had taught her that it was useless, even dangerous, to probe. Nowadays she never asked questions, no matter how late he got home. She always felt certain that he would be by her side in the mornings; he could be so considerate that he often got into bed without waking her, certainly without disturbing her.

When she first woke that morning she couldn't understand the coolness at her back. She turned her head, and saw his empty pillow. It was so smooth that she knew he hadn't been to bed at all, although it was broad daylight. She stretched out a bare arm for the bedside clock, to turn it round so that she could see it more clearly; it was nearly a quarter to eight. She took a few minutes to wake up properly, and then hitched herself up in bed. It was still strange not to look down and see Lionel, grubby and dirty because he always needed a shave so badly in the mornings—he used an electric razor and had never really learned how to shave properly with it.

Ruth Endicott pushed back the sheet and got out of bed, catching a glimpse of herself in the tall wall mirror which Lionel had placed there when getting the house ready. He insisted on her wearing only one of the new fashioned, very short pyjama suits, without the pants; and if he was awake when she got up, he liked to lie there and look at her and also her reflection when she first got out of bed. She did not realise that it was simply by habit that she now sat on the side of the bed and unfastened the ribbon-tapes of the jacket at the neck, where they were loosely tied, and slipped the jacket off her shoulders. She always had a moment's sensuous pleasure when she saw herself like that, knowing that her body was seductively beautiful. Sometimes she even got a thrill out of the way Lionel edged towards her, and from the expression

on his face. At those moments his lips were always moist;
he drooled.

She stretched, yawned, tapped her mouth, and then
stretched out for her panties, bra and slip. She went along to
the bathroom, which had been installed before they had moved
in. Very few houses in Brasher's Row boasted a bathroom.
She had acquired another habit, of a quick morning bath while
the kettle came to the boil on a low gas.

She went downstairs, stark naked because it was so warm.
The storm had lasted over a day, and wind cut along the street
and hissed in at a top window which was not curtained off. She
saw rain and heard it spattering as she put on the kettle. There
was no sign of Lionel, and uneasily she thought that the storm
must have kept him away. She wasn't exactly frightened then,
just uneasy, and it wasn't until she was in the bath that she
admitted the truth to herself.

Whenever Lionel got in very late, or whenever his normal
morning routine was disturbed, he was likely to get vicious.
That wasn't always the case, but it very often was. She tidied
the kitchen quickly, put the breakfast things ready, and hurried upstairs, in case he came back soon. He would expect
everything to be exactly as he liked it; if the breakfast wasn't
ready except for cooking bacon and eggs, he was liable to start
knocking her about. She wondered whether she should have
her bath, decided to risk it, bathed very quickly in tepid water,
and then hurried to the bathroom, putting on her bra as she
went. Twenty minutes after waking, she was downstairs
again, making the tea. Now that she was fully awake she
realised how violent the storm had been; like Lionel's temper.

At nine o'clock, she was too hungry to wait any longer. She
cooked her own breakfast, and dawdled over it. She felt better
then, and began to tell herself what she would do if he started
to get violent. She often had these rehearsals beforehand,
imagining what she would say, how she would hit him back; but
in fact he always terrified her the moment he raised his voice.

It was half past nine when she had finished, and she went
to the front door to bring the milk in. As she did so, a gust of
wind nearly pulled the door out of her grasp, and rain splashed

over her face. She snatched up the milk, backed into the narrow hallway with it, and tried to close the door, but the wind made it difficult, and it wouldn't latch. When at last she closed it, she was breathing hard. To make the situation worse, she had put the milk on the floor behind her and as she turned round she knocked it over; milk spilled out in a huge river and a big pool. In vexation, she stamped in it and made matters worse by splashing the walls. She scurried along to the kitchen for a floorcloth, and was on her knees, swabbing up the mess, when the door began to open.

On the instant, she was terrified; if Lionel came in and caught her doing this, there was no telling what he would do. He couldn't have come at a worse moment. She knelt transfixed, floorcloth in hand and dripping milk, and staring up as the door banged back.

It wasn't Lionel.

It was a man she had never seen before, a youthful-looking man, his plastic raincoat streaming with water, his cloth cap dripping, his brown shoes oozing. He tried to slam the door, but it blew back in his face. He had to struggle with it, as Ruth had, and surprise helped her to relax, even to get angry. What did he mean, opening the door with a key and bursting in like this? She got to her feet, and dripped the milk-soaked cloth into the pail. When he closed the door and turned round, she was facing him.

"Who are you?" she demanded. "What are you doing with a key to my door?"

He didn't answer at once.

In a way, he was quite good-looking, although he was too fat. The wind had whipped colour to his cheek, and his eyes were clear, too; honey brown in colour. He was half smiling, half sneering; Ruth had a vague feeling now that she had seen him before somewhere, but couldn't be sure.

"Go on, answer me! When my husband comes back——"

"Forget it, Ruth," said the man. "Li won't be back, you've got to get used to the idea. He won't be back. He's gone on a long, long journey. I want a little talk with you about him?"

"What do you mean?" she managed to gasp. "What do you mean, he won't come back? Of course he'll come back. He never——"

"Ruth," said the stranger, "he's had trouble. You could have a lot of trouble, too. Don't make any mistake about that. Where does he keep his books and papers—his betting slips, that kind of thing?"

"In—in the living-room. But what——"

"Lead the way," the stranger ordered, and he moved nearer and took her wrist in a firm grip, then twisted her round so that she went ahead of him. As the man pushed her towards the living-room, she knew fear much greater than the fear which possessed her when her husband went berserk. He glanced round, holding her arm up behind her, not hurting but making it obvious that he could hurt at any moment. He stood looking round at the spotless tablecloth, the table ready for Lionel's breakfast, the range of domestic luxuries just visible in the converted wash-house beyond. The man looked round, then took off the raincoat and his cap. He handed them to her.

"Let these drip, baby."

"Look here, I want to know——"

"I told you, Ruth," said the man, "Lionel's had trouble and you can run into plenty of it if you're not careful. Just do what I tell you."

She took the coat and cap into the kitchen, and hung them behind a door. When she got back into the room, the man was standing over the little writing bureau where Lionel kept all his papers.

"Got a key?" the man demanded.

"No, and if I had I wouldn't let you have——" Ruth began, and then stopped, catching her breath; for the stranger turned round and looked at her in a way which frightened her just as much as Lionel ever had.

He said: "Where's the key?"

"I—I haven't got one, Lionel never let me have one! He told me to keep away from that desk, it was private. I—I don't know where a key is."

"You're telling me you've never opened it when he's been out?"

"Of course I haven't! Lionel would have had the skin off my back if he—if he'd thought I'd do a thing like that!" She was beginning to fight for breath.

"That's good," said the man. "That's very satisfactory. If that's true it might help you a lot."

She didn't ask him what he meant, just stood gasping for breath. He took out a big pocket knife, opened a blade, and began to work on the lock. She had heard about locks being picked, but had never seen it done before. In about three minutes there was a loud click, and the middle drawer opened. The man pulled out the other drawers, too, and then opened his case and put most of the papers from Lionel's desk into it. She began to utter a protest; he just turned round and looked at her. When the desk was empty of everything except one bundle of papers, a few sheets of notepaper, pens and pencils and ink and blotting paper, he closed it again and turned round and stared at her. Her fear rose to shrieking point.

"Ruth," he said, "I've got bad news for you. Lionel's dead. He got mixed up with the police, and he was on the run. He was okay while he was free from the cops, but if they'd caught him he would have squealed, so some old pals of his sent him on that long journey."

"Li—Lionel *dead*," she echoed weakly.

She was startled, not yet shocked, and in a peculiar, guilty way, relieved. Lionel *dead*. For a moment she felt quite light-hearted. The implications of what the man was saying did not seem important at first, except the one positive statement.

"Now listen to me," the man went on. "Lionel had a bit put away, four or five thousand quid, judging from these papers." He tapped the documents which he had left behind. "Did a bit of good work on the gee-gees, he knew form all right. Very smart, Lionel was. And you're his next of kin and only heir, so that means you get all the money. And you get this house and all that goes with it."

She was thinking: "Yes, he's right, I get everything." Lionel had no relations except some uncles and aunts he hadn't seen for years, and they would have no claim. She was rich!

"So if you do what you're told, you'll be sitting pretty," the man said. "How much did Lionel tell you about his business?"

"Nothing, I tell you!"

He put his head on one side.

"Don't start lying to me, Ruth."

"But I'm not lying. I asked him about it once, I asked him where he spent all his time, and—and he lammed into me, I was black and blue all over. I didn't dare to ask him any more, and I didn't dare try to look at that desk, either. If he was working at it, I had to be in the kitchen or in the front room or upstairs, he used to make me stay out. Sometimes he'd even send me to the pictures when he was very busy."

"Well, that's fine," said the stranger, and his smile looked very bright and satisfied. "That's what he always told us, that he didn't let you know anything about what he did. And you still don't know anything, do you?" He paused; it seemed for a long time. He moved, slowly, and came towards her. His smile remained, but it was stiff and mirthless; suddenly she was in even greater terror. The man stretched out his hands towards her, and she backed away, knocked against a chair, and fell back on to it. The chair rocked but did not fall. She couldn't get further away, just put up her hands to try to fend him off, but she knew that she would be so helpless against him as she was against Lionel.

"Ruthie," he said very softly, "five thousand pounds, this little house, and a nice quiet peaceful life—how do you like the look of it?"

"It—it sounds wonderful."

"Wonderful," the man said. "That's about right. You can give yourself a good time. You can eat, drink, be merry, and sleep with who you like—if you do what you're told. If you don't, you'll be buried with poor old Lionel."

"Don't talk like that!"

"Listen to me," the man said again, and now he leaned forward and took her wrists, holding them firmly. "The police will catch up with this house soon—perhaps this morning, perhaps tonight, perhaps tomorrow. They'll come and ask you a lot of questions. They'll want to know all you can tell them about Lionel and his pals, and his work. If you don't know anything you can't tell them anything, can you?"

"I swear I don't know anything!"

"Ruthie, if Lionel ever told you a thing, forget it. Just tell the police what you've told me. If you tell them anything that will help them to find Lionel's pals——"

"But I don't know any of his pals!"

"If you don't, you can't name them and you can't come to any harm," said the stranger. "Don't tell the police I came, either. Don't tell them a thing. If you do, I'll find out. Rather than let the cops cut you up in the witness box, I'd cut your throat. Don't make any mistake, Ruthie."

"I swear I can't tell them anything," she gabbled, brokenly. "How can I tell them what I don't know?"

"Okay, Ruthie," the man said. "But don't make any mistake. If I find out that you've told them anything——"

He drew his finger across his throat.

.   .   .   .   .

In a telephone kiosk, twenty minutes later, the man said smoothly:

"She doesn't know a thing, there's no need to worry about her. . . . Listen, Shell, I had to find out. . . . I could tell whether she was lying or not. Now be yourself. She's got to live until she's got her hands on Lionel's dough. It won't take long to separate her from it, and after that. . . . I tell you she's too scared to talk to the cops. They're not going to weep about Li, anyway, they'll be glad he's gone. Leaving Ruthie until I can cash in is playing it smart. . . . Listen, Shell, there isn't a thing more to worry about, but we must lay off for a few weeks. We can afford to. Get some more ideas, maybe. . . . Yes, I know I'm the ideas man: give me a chance, I'm as anxious to get further into the big money as you are. Don't worry, Shell."

He rang off a few moments later, wiped the sweat off his

forehead, and stepped out of the kiosk into the bluster of the warm summer storm.

At Brasher's Row, Ruth Endicott sat and waited.

It was evening before the dreaded moment arrived, and the police car stopped outside the door. She was in the bedroom, sitting at the window; she had been there much of the day. She knew that the important thing was to make the police think she knew nothing about Lionel's death, but she didn't know whether she would be able to hold out. If she didn't, she believed that the stranger would carry out his threat.

VII

LYING WIFE?

THE woman was scared when Roger arrived; there was no doubt about that. The problem was to decide what she was scared about. She was rather small, rather plump, with an incredibly tiny waist and what his sons would call a dreamboat figure. She wore a cotton dress high at the neck, which seemed to mock at modesty because of the bulge below it. She was fair-haired, and had nice china blue eyes and a beautifully smooth complexion. On the back of her left hand was an ugly scar, about two inches long. The little house was spotless, and furnished in a way which very few people who lived in Brasher's Row could afford. Roger tried to make up his mind the best way to approach Endicott's widow, and decided, as often in the past, that he would have to shock her, perhaps cruelly, to loosen her tongue.

"I don't understand. I don't know what you're doing here," she said, running the words into one another. "My husband hasn't got into trouble, has he?"

"Why should you think he has?" demanded Roger.

"I didn't say that, but what else can I think, with you coming up here, and him being away all day? What's the matter? What's happened?" She caught her breath, and then her eyes seemed to light up and she went on with a rush: "He hasn't met with an accident, has he?"

Roger said: "A kind of accident. He was murdered early this morning."

"*Murdered!*"

She brought the word out explosively, as if astounded, but that didn't get rid of the brightness in her eyes. That convinced Roger that she knew the truth already, and that something he had said had pleased her. He began questioning her, slowly and deliberately, but as the minutes slipped by he realised that she was much tougher than she looked.

She swore that she hadn't known where her husband had been all night; that she knew nothing about his business; that she knew none of his friends. She said that he had occasionally been out all night, so she hadn't been surprised this time. She admitted, almost as if it were against her will, that after he was out all night he often came back and gave her a very bad time; she said that was why she had been frightened when he, Roger, had arrived. That could even explain why her eyes had brightened at the prospect of her husband having met with an accident—and explain why she hadn't been appalled at the news that he had been murdered.

For three hours, on and off, Roger questioned her; and she gave the same answers. She didn't know where her husband went, what he did for a living, whom he worked with—he left her at home all the time, he didn't mix business with pleasure. There was obviously a great deal of basic truth in all her answers, while neighbours corroborated much that she said. Three of these testified that they knew how Lionel had beaten her up from time to time.

Roger had a feeling of acute frustration when he left, at nearly ten o'clock that night. He felt sure that the girl was lying part of the time, that there was a great deal which she could tell him—but he had a feeling, too, that she would be able to maintain this steely resistance for as long as she wanted to.

She identified Lionel Endicott's body, without showing much emotion; and the final moment came when she told Roger flatly that she couldn't help it, she was glad her husband was dead.

"Now perhaps I'll get a bit of peace," she said.

.   .   .   .   .

"I don't know what to make of it," Roger said to Bellew, "but I'm going to have the Division watch her for a few weeks. If she's under pressure, or if she's playing any part in the racket, someone will contact her—if they haven't already."

"Daresay you're right," Bellew said. "I've checked Stone's movements, by the way. A dozen witnesses would swear he was two miles away at the time of the murder."

It was at half past two next morning that Roger pulled up outside the shop in Kemp Road, Clapham. The Stone delivery van was parked away from the corner, and some grocery orders were already piled up in cartons inside.

The morning papers had carried the news of Endicott's death, and the *Echo* especially had screeched delight because of the likeness between the artist's drawing and the photograph of the murderer. But the smash-and-grab raid, as well as the discovery of two corpses chained back to back in a cellar in a derelict house, took most of the newspaper space. Casual references were made to Endicott's being a gang killing, but only one newspaper referred to the possibility that the murder of Mrs. Stone might have repercussions. The general attitude was that Endicott had been paid for his crime with a kind of rough justice.

Old Mrs. Klein, wearing a starched white smock, was at the provisions counter, cutting up cheese with a wire. A thin, very plain girl with a hooked nose but a mop of the most lovely chestnut hair, was serving an elderly man with biscuits. The door of the shop leading to the living-room was open, and Stone appeared. He stopped short at sight of Roger.

"Will you come back here, please?" said Stone. He kept the door open, and Roger stepped over the patch where the blood and treacle had mixed, and then into the room, which looked exactly as it had when he had first seen it. Stone closed the door. He was wearing a khaki coat, obviously freshly washed and pressed. He was pale, but his face had a strong look about it. There was calmness in his eyes, too.

"I take it that you've seen the newspapers," Roger said.

"Yes, Mr. West, I have."

"We're quite sure that the dead man was your wife's murderer," Roger said.

"I daresay you are, Mr. West."

"I don't want you to be in any doubt," Roger went on, but he felt much the same as he had when he had talked to Endicott's wife last night, frustrated, even a little angry. "I've brought photographs of Endicott's head and shoulders from the back, and close-up of his face. And I've brought enlargements of the prints found in this room last Friday." He opened his briefcase, took out the photographs, and spread them on the sideboard for Stone to examine. Stone looked at them all with close interest, and then said:

"I don't doubt that's the man, Mr. West."

"Do you recognise the face?"

"Yes, I do."

"That's good," Roger said. He felt the barrier of resistance even more strongly, and was fully convinced that Stone was holding something back. He hoped to make the man talk more freely as he said: "I was afraid that you would go chasing shadows. I didn't want there to be the slightest doubt about this man's identity."

"There isn't any," Stone said. "Are there any more formalities, Mr. West?"

"There will be some, but they're not urgent," Roger answered. The odd thing was that he didn't quite know what to say next; it was like boxing a shadow. "Is there anything you want to ask me?"

"There is one thing, apart from thanking you for being so considerate about it all."

"Forget that. What's the one thing?"

"I've spent a lot of time with old newspapers in the Public Library," went on Stone, "and I've been studying all the robberies at shops like mine. There have been a lot of them, haven't there?"

Roger thought: "Oh." He hesitated, trying to make sure of the best way to answer; he plumped for complete frankness. "Yes, far too many."

"And this man Endicott was murdered, wasn't he?"

"Yes."

"Do you know who killed him?"

"Not yet, but we soon shall."

"It won't help you much if someone else kills *his* murderer when you catch up with him, will it?" asked Stone, and bitterness forced its way through his enforced calm. "This is the question I want to ask you, Mr. West: do you believe that these robberies are organised by the same people?"

Roger said, very slowly, very carefully: "I've considered the possibility, and so have some of my colleagues, but there isn't any evidence except that which you've been able to deduce from the newspapers. We have the same information in more detail, that's all. There are indications that the thefts could be organised, but it's at least as possible that the only real connection is the fence, or receiver——"

"I know what a fence is."

"Then you may know that crooks who specialise in the same kind of stolen goods often use the same fence—and in this case the fence is probably someone who can find an easy outlet for cigarettes. But even that's guesswork, and we've certainly no evidence."

"But you, personally, think there could be a connection between all these crimes?" asked Stone.

"Obviously there could be."

"Thank you very much, Mr. West," said Stone. "That's all I wanted to ask you."

It would be possible to keep on questioning him, but he was quite as stubborn as Lionel Endicott's widow. In their way, they had a lot in common and temperamentally they seemed very much alike.

Roger said: "Let me know at any time if I can help, will you? I won't be handling the rest of the formalities myself, Mr. Bellew will do that, or one of his men. But I'll always be available on the telephone."

"Thank you, Mr. West," Stone said.

He did not offer to shake hands.

Roger felt the disappointing gaze of Mrs. Klein, and the interest of the auburn haired girl with that absurdly hooked nose, as he went out of the shop. Stone politely opened the door for him. Roger got into his car, reversed into Middleton Street, and by the time he was driving off, Stone was carrying more cartons of groceries to his van. It was a strangely unsatisfactory climax, or anti-climax, and he was no happier about this man than he was about Endicott's widow.

He drove to the Clapham Police Station and went up to Bellew's office. Bellew, in his shirt sleeves, was studying a map

of his big, sprawling Division, and in his mouth he held half
a dozen pins with red heads. "'Arfaminnit," he mumbled, and
consulted a paper on his desk, stuck two pins into the map,
studied the paper again and stuck in another pin, then spat the
others out into the huge palm of his hand, and said: "Sorry,
Handsome. Had a proper crop of burglaries last night. Fourteen, and looks as if half of them were done by the same crowd,
too."

"Want any help?" Roger asked.

"Dunno yet," said Bellew. "What can I do for you this
morning?"

"I've just seen young Stone," Roger told him. "I fancy it
would be a good idea to keep an eye on him for the next few
weeks. He thinks Endicott may have been killed to keep him
quiet, and he's pretty deep."

"He'll soon forget it," said Bellew, over-confidently. "I'll
tell my chaps to keep an eye on him, though." He glanced at
the map, as if he much preferred to think about the crop of
robberies. "Any luck from the Old Man about checking up
on the possibility of an organised shop robbery racket?"

The truth was that with the murderer dead, Bellew himself
wasn't deeply interested; as a Divisional Superintendent he
had to worry about the crimes under his nose, and there were
plenty.

"Not yet," said Roger.

"Lemme know if I can help," said Bellew, absently.

"Jack."

"Yep?"

"Once every week or two I'll look in and collect the latest
report on Jim Stone," Roger said. "Don't let it get lost in a
filing cabinet, will you?"

Bellew grinned.

"Tell you another thing," Roger said. "Endicott's widow
might know a lot more than we realise, so I'm going to get
Charlie Baker to keep an eye on her, too."

For the first time, Bellew looked as if he were really giving
Roger his full attention, and his gaze did not stray to the map
or to the red-headed pins now on his desk. He began to smile,

and sat back in his chair, looking enormous against the pale green background of the bare wall.

"Just warning me that you're not going to be put off, eh? Never mind what the A.C. and the Commander say, you're more on the ball than they are, and you're going to find out what's going on. Right?"

"So long as we understand each other."

Bellew gave a deep, half-amused laugh.

"Be damned difficult not to understand what you mean, Handsome, but okay—I'll see that Stone's watched for the next few weeks. That's a promise. I suppose the truth is that I doubt if we'll get much in the way of shop robberies for a while, especially if they really are organised. Last night's crop of bad men got me on the raw. Got anybody with you on this?"

"Dr. Appleby."

"If you two can't get to the bottom of it, no one can," said Bellew, picking up the pins again. "Now if it's all the same to you, I'll get some work done."

VIII

DOUBTS

FOR the next three weeks, news of shop robberies attracted Roger as aniseed attracts bloodhounds, but even his application to them began to slacken after the three weeks. There was a fair crop of such robberies, mostly sneak-thefts, nearly all carried out when an elderly person or a woman was alone in a shop, but in no single case during that period was anyone hurt. Five men were clearly described by the shopkeepers, and three of these were later picked up by the Divisional police, while the police also arrested four others, from fingerprints or habit-methods recognised at the scenes of the crimes. None of these robberies was sensational. A few similar crimes were committed up and down the country, but there was nothing like enough to make a sensation. As the Yard had no official view on the possibility of an organised ring, no request for information about similar crimes went out to the other boroughs or the provinces, but Roger wrote to a dozen police chiefs whom he knew well, asking them to keep him informed. In Edinburgh and in Newcastle a shop robbery with violence took place, in both places the assailant was found; there was no evidence that either worked for a gang.

Any reference to such robberies at the Yard was made with snide looks at Roger. Bellew adopted a long-suffering air when Roger made his weekly call, and Charlie Baker of the White-chapel Division had nothing to report about Endicott's wife.

Then, an odd little thing happened.

Jim Stone went away for three days, without telling the girl at the shop where he was going. Bellew's men reported this, and the police made discreet inquiries; Stone had told the girl that he had some "business" to look after. After three days he came back and resumed work in exactly the way he had before his wife's death.

"They say he never smiles, never says anything except in

the way of business," Bellew told Roger. "I'm beginning to get as worried about him as you are, Handsome."

"Nice to know you'll keep watching him," Roger said, but apart from the fact that it added to the disquiet that he felt about the man, nothing developed.

On that same day, he drove the long way round to Chelsea, from Clapham, going past River View Hostel and then over Battersea Bridge. Kings Road was up for electricity repairs so he had to make a detour. On the corner of one of the little streets along which he drove was a grocery and provision shop, rather like Stone's. The name on the front was Marsh, a fact which Roger noticed in the way he was likely to notice any little fact which came his way; he would probably forget it, but one day some incident might dig it out of his mind.

He went home, to find Martin and Richard sparring together in the back garden, wearing boxing gloves. He watched for ten minutes, marvelling that two "babies" of what seemed like yesterday were now tall and husky; marvelling even more that Richard, who had once been so much smaller, was now at least as tall as Martin, although Martin was the broader. They were high-spirited and happy, until Martin caught Richard on the mouth, and drew blood. Janet called out of the kitchen:

"I *knew* you'd hurt each other. You know I hate boxing, too. For goodness sake, Roger, don't stand there like a big boy, come in and get your supper."

Martin winked; Richard called: "I'm all right, Mum," and Roger said:

"Won't be a minute, sweet. Let me have your gloves, Fish, I'll teach old Scoop."

.   .   .   .   .

Violet Marsh was alone in her shop when the Wests were fooling about in the garden.

The grocery and provisions side was closed, but they had built a little kiosk, with a separate service door and window, for cigarettes and sweets; and this part of the shop was open at half past six. It was a dead hour when Violet usually wheeled herself about the shop, studying the shelves, making sure what goods ought to be brought up from the cellar next morning. A few people on the way to the pictures would look in for cigarettes or sweets or chocolates, not really enough to make it economic to keep open. But for Violet, this was the most important hour of the day.

She was on her own, and no one would ever realise what it meant to be back in complete charge. Before the motor accident, in which her husband had been killed, she had run the shop almost single-handed. Now, without legs, she could not hope to. Her sister and brother-in-law had taken over, and did a good job, but Violet had been away for nearly a year and it wasn't reasonable that they would do everything her way. They were good-natured and good-hearted, however, and gradually Violet was reassuming some kind of control—building up shelf stocks, for instance, checking how much of particular goods had been sold during the previous day, noting it down on the little clip-board which she kept fastened to the arm of her wheel-chair. She could manoeuvre that chair about skilfully, now, and run behind all the counters, serving everything except the goods kept on the top shelves.

She was counting the sugar when a man opened the door leading to the small part of the shop. Sugar was always a problem for storage, and the profit on it was small. Almost with relief, she swung her chair round, wheeled herself out of the main shop, and smiled at the man standing at the counter. He was rather short, he needed a shave, and he wore a peak cap which he kept low over his eyes.

"Good evening, sir," Violet Marsh said.

"Ten *Mediums*," the man ordered; his voice was gruff and almost unpleasant. Violet had never seen him before, but did not give a thought to possible danger. She turned her chair round and stretched out for the cigarettes, making a mental note that the sale of *Mediums* was undoubtedly on the way up—although once a current television advertising programme stopped, sales might fall back to the old level. She heard a movement behind her, but paid no attention; it needed only a second or two to get the cigarettes.

As she turned back, she saw the man's hand sweeping towards her, in it a tin of toffees. She had no time to scream. She opened her mouth as the tin caught her on the forehead. She flung up her hands, but he smashed them down and struck her again, this time a swinging blow on the other side of the face. The first blow had sent the chair against the shelves behind her, the second caught her at such an angle that the wheel-chair, its brake off, rolled along the corridor behind the counter, taking the man completely by surprise. Violet was in pain, but conscious; and she realised exactly what had happened. She saw the man scramble over the counter after her, saw the malevolence in his eyes and the way his little teeth showed. He grabbed a bottle of lemon squash from a pile, and a dozen other bottles fell, crashing and clanking.

Violet dropped her hands to the wheels of the chair and spun them with the skill of constant practice. As the man landed behind the counter, she went hurtling back towards the main shop, the door to which was wide open, for easy access.

The man flung the bottle at her. It hurtled straight towards her face. She snatched one hand off a wheel and took the force of the missile, which struck the bone of her wrist and caused great pain, numbing the whole arm. But it did not alter the speed or direction of the chair, which went sailing through the open door, and almost with a reflex action, she swung out her sound arm, caught the door, and slammed it.

She was sobbing, gasping. She had no time to lock the door, and the man must be just behind it. Somehow she managed to make the numbed hand work, and spun the wheels so that the chair swung round in a half circle, then rolled towards the door which led to the kitchen. Now she was screaming all the time, but her mind was working, and suddenly an idea swept into it. She couldn't get out of this shop, for the other door was closed; and the man would be in at any moment. But at her hand were bottles of ammonia, bottles of carbolic acid and other chemicals for domestic use. She swung the chair behind the counter, and the door opened. She snatched a bottle off the right shelf without being sure what it was, and hurled it at the man. He had a bottle of fruit squash in his hand, and raised it to protect himself. The bottle she had thrown smashed against his, and broke—and in front of her eyes, in an awful moment, she saw his malevolent expression fade, saw horror replace it, saw his mouth open wide in a shuddering breath, then heard him scream. She realised that the acid has splashed his face. She saw him stagger, turn and run. Once, she thought he would fall, but he steadied himself against the counter in the kiosk, and went forward again.

She sat there gasping for breath, blood dripping from two wounds in her face, her wrecked body numbed, her mind filled with dread. She did not know how long it was before a customer from along the street came in, and saw her through the open door.

. . . . .

Richard's lips were a little swollen, but not badly hurt. Roger's right eye had a slight red contusion, where Martin-called-Scoopy had managed to catch him with a left hook. Martin, tonight, was unmarked. All their high spirits were back, Janet was over her annoyance, and the boys were devouring a gooseberry pie in the dining-room of the house in Bell Street, Chelsea. It was warm. All three "men" were in their shirt sleeves, Janet wore a sleeveless dress which had seen many better days; it was a little too tight for her, and a little too low at the back.

"Dad, give me a straight answer, will you?" asked Scoopy. He was poker-faced, which gave a hint that something offbeat was coming. Janet studied his broad, strong face, which could break so easily into a broad smile—and would show the slightly grey tooth which he had nearly lost in a boxing match at his school.

"If it deserves one," Roger said.

"What do you honestly think about Mum's dress? I mean, if you saw a girl walking along the street with a skin-tight dress like that, poking out in all the proper places, wouldn't you think——?"

Richard roared.

"Don't you talk about my clothes like that," Janet said, half laughing, half vexed.

It would be easy to say the wrong thing, Roger sensed—to turn a happy supper table into one near the edge of discord. Quickly aware that perhaps it wasn't so funny, Richard smothered his laughter. Scoopy, doubting the success of the joke, sat straight-faced. All of them waited for Roger, and he finished a spoonful of pie, put his head on one side and looked Janet up and down, then said lightly:

"If you chaps marry a girl who keeps her figure half as long as your mother has, you'll be lucky."

Janet's eyes kindled.

"Good old Dad," applauded Richard.

"I'd better get out of here and go and do some prep. before I really put my foot right in it," said Scoopy. He pushed his chair back, moved towards the door, turned round and placed his capable hands firmly on Janet's bare arms, close to the shoulders, and blew down her back. "Sorry, Mum, but how about a trip to Mr. Marks's Emporium?" He gave her a quick squeeze, winked at his father over her head, and went out.

Richard began to clear away the supper things, tonight his brother's job, but he took it on himself so as to be sure that no tempers were ruffled; Richard was an inveterate peace-maker. As he went into the kitchen with a load of dirty dishes, Janet said:

"He *is* seventeen, I suppose. What were you like when you were seventeen?"

"I haven't changed a bit," Roger declared.

"No, you ass——"

The telephone bell rang, and Roger shifted his chair and stretched out for the extension in this room; only a few months ago he had arranged for this extension, and that had been a tacit acceptance of the fact that they were likely to be in this house for another few years. They had lived here since they had married, twenty-two years ago.

"Roger West," Roger said.

"If it's the Yard, tell them no," whispered Janet.

"Yes, speaking," said Roger; and then Janet saw his expression change, and could tell that this was a job which really affected him. "Where?" he asked, and slipped a pencil out of a drawer on the telephone table and began to write. "Yes, I've got it. How is she . . .? Yes, of course. . . . Yes, I'll ring him." He rang off, studied the address, and said in an aside to Janet: "Do you know that shop at the corner of Ashley and Kebble Streets—Marsh's?"

"I know there's one there," Janet said. "I don't think I've ever been in it, but I think it's where a woman was badly injured in a car accident, and her husband died. Something like that. She was crippled, too."

"And now she's at death's door," Roger said.

"A—shop robbery?"

Roger was dialling Dan Appleby's number; and he nodded.

Janet said, in a husky voice: "Somehow it never seems real when you read about it in the papers, but when it happens so near at hand——" She broke off, as Richard appeared at one door and Scoopy at the other, both intensely interested.

"Got a nasty job, Dad?" inquired Richard.

"There's been a shop robbery in Chelsea, and the woman is badly hurt," Janet said. "Don't worry your father, now." She got up, and each of them came in and took something off the table and went into the kitchen. Roger was talking. "It's a shop in Ashley Street, or——"

"*Marsh's?*" exclaimed Scoopy.

"Yes."

"Not old Ma Marsh," Richard said, in a shocked voice. "Why, that's where——" he broke off.

"A lot of us go there for our tuck. It's not far from the school, and—well, one of the sons used to be at the Comprehensive School," said Scoop. "Good Lord. What swine these chaps are."

They heard the telephone ting, as Roger finished. Janet said: "Stay here," and went to the door. They watched her as she disappeared, and heard her say:

"Are you going, darling?"

"Must do."

"I expect you'll be late," Janet said. "At least you've had supper."

"Dad!" called Richard. "Shall I go and open the garage door?"

IX

CERTAINTY

"THE game old duck," said Dan Appleby. "So she sprayed him with a good corrosive." He was standing near the place from which Mrs. Marsh had thrown the bottle, and watching the Divisional and the Yard men at work. "What have you done, Handsome?"

"Alerted all London for a man splashed with the acid," Roger said. "It shouldn't be long before we pick him up. I've told all hospitals, all doctors are being telephoned, and unless he finds a doctor who'll patch him up without saying anything, we should have news within an hour. From what I've been able to see of the amount that came out of the bottle, he must be in a bad way."

"Full bottle, broken," said Appleby. "Shattered, in fact." He looked down at the thick brown glass, the bottom of the bottle, which had only an inch of dark brown liquid in it. His gaze travelled round to the shelves and to the floor. "You'll be doing me out of a job, soon," he said. "Not much on the floor, not much on the shelves—he must have been smothered with the stuff." He stepped over some broken glass, and looked at a spot on a shelf at about chest level. "See that lot?"

"Looks to me as if he defended himself with a bottle at about face level," Roger reasoned. "That's the place you would try to protect. The acid went over him but a good heavy splash reached there." He pointed to the spot which Dan Appleby was already contemplating.

"Looks to me as if it went fairly straight," said Appleby. "See that dent in the tin of Golden Syrup? Fancy coming across that stuff again. Where the rounded edge of the bottle struck the tin, no scratch or jag marks, just a dent. How's the injured woman?"

"They think she'll pull through," Roger said. "Will you let me know what you think, when you've seen her?"

"Right away," promised Appleby. "And let me know when you've found the chap."

.   .   .   .   .

That night Adam Gantry was paying for all the viciousness, all the devilry, all the sadism, which was in his nature, for not only was the back of his right hand a terrible mass of acid burns, but his right cheek had a big blistering burn in it, which seemed to be eating right through to the other side, to his mouth. There were also spots of burning all over his face and wrists, a smear on his forehead, and a tiny spot which was excruciatingly painful in the corner of his left eye.

He staggered out of the Marsh shop, mouth wide open, taking in great gulps of air. His one good eye was all right, and he saw that the street was empty. He turned the corner. His motor-scooter was parked where he had left it, the light still on. He staggered towards it, sat astride, and started the engine; it ticked over at once. He did not think consciously about the danger of driving in his condition, all he realised was that he had to get away from the spot, and had to get a doctor. There was one, Carmody, who worked for the gang; if he could only reach Carmody he would be all right.

He swerved round the corner. A motorist's horn blared at him. He reached the main road and turned into it more cautiously. He must get over the river, drive to Lambeth, then on to the Old Kent Road, where Carmody lived. All he could think about was the pain and the doctor. *Carmody, Carmody, Carmody.*

Wind bit at the burns on his face, and his whole head seemed to be afire. He did not think he could get as far as Carmody's place. Then—then he must have help. What did you do with acid burns? He had used nearly every kind of weapon, every kind of brutality, but not acid. *What did one do for acid?* He turned right and then left, and found himself on the Embankment. The shadowy figure of a policeman loomed up, and he slowed down a little, gasping, trying to be sure that he did not attract the man's attention. He passed. *What did one do for acid?*

He saw a telephone kiosk, its light on, not far away; at a corner. There was little traffic. Gasping in his agony, he stopped the machine and propped it up against the kerb, then staggered towards the telephone booth. He pulled it open, and stepped inside. He put his left hand, the uninjured hand, to his trousers pocket, and had to move the coat aside; as he touched his coat the tip of his forefinger began to burn. He snatched it away, realising that there was acid on his coat. He was sobbing. He managed to drag out four coppers, got them into the slot, and with the middle finger of his right hand dialled the number he knew, the contact number for serious trouble: Whitechapel 84312. Once his finger slipped, and he was terrified in case he should have to do it all over again, but he heard the ringing sound.

A man said: "This is Fats."

"Fats," Gantry gasped. "Fats, I—I'm burned bad. Acid. I gotta see Carmody. I'm burned bad. It's awful, God, it's awful. I——"

"I'll get Carmody for you," the man at the other end of the telephone said quickly and crisply. "Where are you?"

"Chelsea—Embankment. Fats, it's awful."

"Yes, but where?"

Cars were passing, there were a few lights on the other side of the river, a boy and a girl walked by, arm-in-arm. Through the kiosk windows on his left Gantry saw a red sign: The Tug.

"Adam, are you there?" demanded the man named Fats sharply.

"There's—a pub. The Tug," Gantry muttered. "Just along—just along from here."

"Okay, Adam," Fats said. "You go to that pub. I know it. There's a parking yard, just behind it. You go and wait there, get behind a car. I won't be long."

"You—you won't—be, will you?" Gantry muttered. "My face is awful. Awful."

"See if you can find some water in the parking place, and rinse your face. That'll help," advised Fats. "Don't rub it, just rinse it."

"O—okay, Fats. You won't be long, will—will you?"

"I'll see that Carmody gets there nearly as soon as you do," promised Fats.

Gantry hung up; even that was an effort. He moved out of the kiosk, missed a step, and saw the red sign, The Tug, between the dark-leafed branches of some trees. He swayed. A couple approaching gave him a wide berth, but he did not realise that they thought he was drunk. He saw the pub across a narrow road, near an intersection where several roads met. He drew himself upright as the breeze tortured his cheeks and his hand; the fingertip was burning terribly. He reached the kerb, crossed it, and saw three people come out of the pub, two of them laughing. They walked off, without noticing him. He saw the entrance to the car park, and staggered towards it; if anyone saw him, they took no notice.

He crossed the road and went into the car park, which was lit by a single low wattage lamp, where moths and insects flew in fluttering panic. A dozen cars were in here—and he saw a water tap in a corner, with a hose snaking from it. He could not get there fast enough. His face, his hands, his body now seemed afire. He hardly remembered what had happened. He bent over the tap, wrenched the hose off, turned the tap full on and held his hands beneath it, cupping them. He splashed water over his face and neck, and it brought a blessed coolness which lasted for a few seconds, so wonderful that he could hardly realise that the pain had been so bad. He kept on splashing. Hands, arms, face, neck—if he could only keep the coolness of the water on them he would be all right. He had to.

The water splashed and squirted over his trousers and his shoes. He turned the tap down a little, but pain surged back. *He couldn't keep on splashing, he just couldn't.* He couldn't keep on his feet, either. He felt his knees buckle, sat down heavily, and discovered that it was easier this way. His head ached less. If he could lie under that tap—that was it, if he could lie *under* that tap, let it run all over him like a shower, it would bring relief all the time, and he would not need to move. He lowered himself to one side, then on to his back, and his back didn't hurt. He hitched himself forward so that the water splashed on to his chin, and he raised his hands so that it sprayed them, too.

He was still in pain, but it was no longer agony, and soon Dr. Carmody would come. There would be no trouble, then. Carmody. Fats wouldn't keep him waiting for long. Fats was a good sort, Fats was. Fats, Carmody. Fats, Carmody.

He saw movement and heard footsteps, opened his eyes but could not see at first because there was such a blur of water in them. Then a man appeared as a misty figure, kneeling down beside him.

"Doc," he muttered. "That you, Doc?"

"It's okay, Adam," said the man named Fats. He was the fattish man who had frightened Ruth Endicott. "You don't have anything more to worry about. Tell me where it hurts." He bent closer, and there was a click of sound, but Adam Gantry did not realise that it was the click of a flick-knife, and he did not see the shimmering blade.

"My face," he muttered. "That eye. My face——"

"Okay, Adam," Fats said. "Forget it now."

Gantry felt a sudden sharp searing pain in his breast, near the heart. He did not know what had happened, he did not know that the man he had thought would rescue him had murdered him.

.   .   .   .   .

Roger was at Marsh's shop when a man came in from the street, a plain-clothes constable from the Division, young enough to show his excitement. He was thin and lanky, and anything but a "typical" policeman.

It was a little before half past ten. Roger had finished all he could do here, and Appleby had been gone for an hour. The other Marshes had been brought back from the cinema where they had gone for the evening, and were shocked and horrified. Now and again Marsh would say: "It's not safe to be in a shop alone—it's not safe. No one cares about the little man, these days, either. The big shops are all right, but the little man . . ."

Roger said to the Detective Constable: "What's making you so happy, Owen?"

"Just had a flash from the Yard, sir, over the radio," the Detective Constable said eagerly. "They've found a man with his face badly burnt, proper mess according to the reports. And that's not all." He did not have the sense to see that Roger was already annoyed by his manner. "Stabbed to death, too."

He broke off, half grinning.

Roger said roughly: "And that's funny? Where is he?"

"I didn't wait to hear——"

"Well go and find out!" roared Roger. "Don't come to me again with half a story!" He watched the man swing round and hurry out, glared, and muttered: "God knows what we're getting in the C.I.D. these days." One of the Yard's Fingerprint men shook his head with mock dismay and a Chelsea Divisional Inspector said: "Go a bit easy with Cyril Owen, Mr. West, will you?"

"Why?" asked Roger.

"He's as keen as they come," the D.I. said. "We don't get many like him these days, and he ought to go a long way. He knows London inside out—he's spent his holidays cycling all over the city ever since he was at school. Be a pity to smack him down too hard, if you don't mind my saying so."

Roger said: "I'm glad to know." He leaned against a counter, hand touching some packets of breakfast cereal, thinking that this must be the final evidence he needed; if the man who had attacked Mrs. Marsh had been murdered to stop him from talking, then there was no longer any doubt about an organised campaign. All his superiors would have to concede its certainty, now, and he would surely get the job of investigating.

It was a hell of a job, too.

Marsh, a small, grey-haired, mild-looking man was saying from the doorway:

"It just isn't safe anywhere these days; they ought to do something about it. What with one thing and another, the little man's finished. That's the truth of it, no one cares about the little man."

Roger fought back the impulse to say: "We'll find this

devil." There was a lot to do, and talk wouldn't help to get it done. Poor little Violet Marsh, legless but so brave, and close to death again; and this little grey-haired man with a mild-mannered wife who said little but was so scared—as was every shop keeper whoever had to be alone in his shop.

How could they all be protected?

In spite of the big chain stores, there were tens of thousands of little men, up and down the country, thousands in London alone—people who preferred their independence to a safe job and steady money.

The Divisional Detective Constable came back, this time frowning as if with bad news, punctilious in the way he drew up before Roger, and obviously worried.

"Well?" Roger asked mildly.

"The body was found in the parking place of a public house, The Tug, in Quay Street near the Chelsea Embankment, sir. The Division has already taken over, much to the annoyance of a dozen people who have their cars there."

"We want them questioned, and then we'll send 'em home." Roger looked round again, and went on to the Divisional Detective Inspector who would be in charge: "If anything else crops up here, let me know at the Tug."

"O.K., Mr. West," the Divisional man said, and Roger went to the door. The Divisional Constable opened it smartly. They stepped outside, and the man stepped briskly to Roger's car and opened the door.

"Get in on the other side," Roger ordered. "Been in the C.I.D. for long?"

"Five days, sir."

"Well, it didn't take you long to learn that when you talk to a Detective Superintendent you don't have to find death funny."

"It won't happen again, sir." When Roger didn't comment, but started the engine, Owen ventured to continue: "Very ugly business, isn't it?"

"It's going to mean a lot of overtime before it's finished," Roger said. "You'd better warn your girl friend."

.   .   .   .   .

There were no distinguishing marks on the dead man's clothes, but there was a curious fatty odour about his coat sleeves, and Roger thought, vaguely, of bacon fat. He couldn't identify it for certain, but was vindicated next day. Among the oddments in the pocket, caught in a hole in the lining, was a little shell—a winkle shell. No one saw any significance in that.

Identification was made by a little old woman, dry-eyed, leathery-skinned, who claimed that this was her son, and claimed also that she did not know anything about his spare-time movements, only that he had a temporary job as a bacon hand at a Cockell shop nearby. A "Cockell" shop was becoming a byword, for Cockell's was a chain of supermarkets opening new stores all over London.

Roger went to see the shop manager. Everything from packaged goods to bacon and milk was sold, and it was a self-service establishment, with the goods displayed for easy handling, and three girl cashiers sitting by their adding machines near the exit. The manager, an elderly man named Pearson, led Roger past dozens of customers who were selecting goods and dropping them into their little baskets.

"Gantry," he said, when they were in his office. "Sit down, Superintendent, do. Gantry—well, I didn't want to employ him. I didn't trust him, as a matter of fact. I knew him in the days when I owned this shop. Couldn't rely on him not to help himself out of the till, but—well, it's not so easy to fiddle the money in these stores, that's one advantage since we were taken over. Everything's so ruthlessly efficient, the little man doesn't get a chance."

He was echoing Marsh's words, and Roger murmured sympathetic understanding.

"And I will say this, Gantry was a good judge of bacon, and a good bacon cutter, although it was the devil's own job to make him wear his white coat. I took him on against my better judgement. We're very short-handed, and it's not easy to turn a man down. But Gantry—well, what a way to end up."

"After robbing a little grocery shop," Roger remarked.

"I always suspected that he took stuff off my shelves," the

manager said. "If he did, he must have known where to dispose of it, Mr. West. But as for who he sold to—I just don't know. If I'd followed my nose, I'd have fired him weeks ago, but—well, it's no use pretending, you must *have* staff. I do hope the woman he attacked will recover."

"The one good thing is that Mrs. Marsh will get over it," Appleby told Roger, the following evening. "Don't know what her mental outlook will be like, but physically she'll recover. Persuaded the Commander that this is organised yet?"

Roger said: "I've put in a request to be assigned to this exclusively, but I haven't had any answer. I quoted you as being in favour."

"I certainly am," Appleby said. He blinked out of the window of Roger's office. "B-b-by the way, my wife doesn't hate you any more. She says she thinks it might be a good idea if we met socially, if you could bear it. Think you and your wife could spare an hour or so Sunday evening? Be very glad if you'd come round for a sandwich supper and a drink."

"We'd like that very much," Roger said.

Appleby gave a boyish grin.

"Thought you would. We can get the little women nattering while we work out this he-man's job, can't we? If you ask me, Handsome, we've a hell of a lot to do. Since you found those acid smears in the telephone kiosk, we can be pretty sure that Gantry phoned from there, and the man he phoned might have come and murdered him. It looks very nasty indeed. How many shops like these in London?"

"There's no record," Roger said. "But there are at least a hundred to every division, and we've forty-two divisions."

"Best hope I can see is the widow of the man Endicott," Appleby said. "Sure she can't tell you any more?"

"Not sure yet," Roger said, "but I am sure that she's being watched by the people who killed her husband, and I wouldn't like her to have her throat cut. As soon as we get a chance, we'll talk to her again, though."

"Good," said Appleby. "Don't forget Sunday. Six-thirty or so, if that's all right with you."

It was then Friday.

On the Saturday morning, a brisk telephone call from the Commander, C.I.D., assigned Roger to the Shop Robberies Investigation, exclusively. From that moment onwards, he could think, talk and act only about small shops and their occupants.

X

SECOND DISAPPEARANCE

ON the Monday morning, after a long evening at the Applebys' in which Janet West and Dot Appleby seemed likely to become good friends, Roger found a pencilled note on his desk: "*Please call Supt. Bellew.*" He didn't put the call in at once, but studied the result of the week-end's work by men assigned with him on the shop robberies job. Each Division had been asked to give the location, name, turnover and opening times of the small neighbourhood shops in the Division, and already three Divisions, who must have worked overtime, had turned in fairly comprehensive statements. He did not like what he saw on these; on one list there were a hundred and twenty-three shops. He telephoned the Map Room, and the Inspector in charge said:

"I got your chit, Handsome—I'll use red-headed pins with a white dot for your shops."

"I'll send some stuff down right away," Roger added. "When will you be ready for me to have a look?"

"Give me two hours."

"That'll do fine," said Roger, and rang off. He checked that there was no further news in about Adam Gantry, and compared notes on this case with notes on Endicott; it was surprising how little the people who had known him seemed to know about his activities. He was looking for cross-references all the time, but found none.

He put in the call to Bellew.

"Morning, Handsome," Bellew said. "No use calling you much before nine, is it? I thought you had a conscience." He did not wait for comment, but went on: "Stone's disappeared again—for five days, this time."

"Without saying where?"

"Without saying a word to anyone," Bellew assured him. "I had a talk with Mrs. Klein on the telephone. She says that he's gone surly with her and everyone else, and some of the customers are complaining. It looks to me as if the death of his wife turned his head a bit."

Roger said: "It could be."

"I don't know how much of it is our business," Bellew went on. "There's no reason why a man shouldn't go off for a few days. If he was still married I'd say that he probably goes off for a few nights on the tiles. Could be that, I suppose—may miss his wife, and have a tart tucked away."

"There was no suggestion of another woman while his wife was alive, was there?"

"Nope."

"Well, he doesn't seem to be the type to be able to fix an affair easily," Roger said. "He may just like getting up and going off on his own. Let me know when he comes back, will you?"

"Yep. Before you go, Handsome——"

"Hmm-hmm?"

"I never knew we had so many little shops in the Division —tucked away on their own, I mean."

"How many?"

"Seventy-eight, mostly general stores, but a few fish and chip shops."

"You're practically free of 'em," Roger declared. "Fulham and Chelsea have a hundred and nine each. You'll draw up your suggestions for keeping yours under surveillance, won't you?"

"Yep," said Bellew, less decisively, and he gave Roger the impression that he was thinking of something else—as if he were sticking pins into a map. "There's one thing, though."

"What's that?"

"We can't do it."

"Can't do what?"

"Watch all those shops properly and do our usual job."

"You think of a way," urged Roger and forced a laugh as he rang off; but he knew that Bellew was right. Every Division had been asked to draw up such a plan of surveillance and most of them would come back with the same comment: "*Impossible*".

It was half past nine. He put in a call to Appleby's flat, and Appleby was soon on the line.

"Morning, Dan," Roger said. "Are you good at psychiatry, too?"

"Becoming schizophrenic?" inquired Appleby. "What's the problem?"

Roger said: "The man Stone has disappeared again, this time for five days. Old Mrs. Klein, who works there with the girl, says that when he's home he has long periods of brooding silence, that he's getting sour and short tempered, and upsetting some of the customers. She says he won't have much to do with his mother—she didn't have any time for his wife, thought he'd married beneath him, and Stone hasn't forgotten that. Is this delayed shock effect?"

"Stone's a doer," Appleby said, without any hesitation. "He's not a sit-and-thinker. He probably blames himself for leaving his wife alone in the shop, and is brooding over revenge. When he goes off he's probably planning to hit back somehow."

Roger said: "But what can he do?"

"Why don't you find a good copper who can follow Stone next time he goes and find out what he's up to?" suggested Appleby. "There must be someone on the Force who can follow without being shaken off."

"Might be a good idea," Roger agreed, thoughtfully. "He knows the Division is watching him, and can dodge their chaps. We'd need someone he doesn't know and wouldn't suspect."

"That's it."

Roger rang off, and sat back in his chair, fiddling with a pencil. Appleby's suggestion was worth trying and he needed a man who didn't look like a policeman, who really knew his way about London, and was keen as mustard on what might prove a dull job. He went over all the men who might fit into this at the Yard, and rejected one after another for a variety of reasons. Then he remembered Detective Constable Owen, who had boobed about the report of Adam Gantry's death. Owen didn't look like the popular conception of a policeman, he was supposed to be mustard keen, and was said to know

London and the East End well. Roger put in a call to the
Chelsea Headquarters, and the Superintendent in charge
said:

"Oh, yes, young Owen's bright enough, and he'd jump at
the chance of being attached to the Yard even temporarily.
But it would be a mistake to smack him down too hard,
Handsome."

"You chaps stick together, don't you?"

"If he slips up——"

"I'll send him over to you for reprimand," Roger said. He
rang off a few minutes later, after arranging for Owen to come
to the Yard during the afternoon.

It was less than two hours since the Chief Inspector in the
Map Room had spoken to him, but when he went down there,
Roger saw at once that the Division so far covered by reports
had been marked up on the big detailed maps on the walls.
Several big mobile screens had a map on each side. The red
pins with white dots were mixed with pins of all colours,
covering accidents, household burglaries, house-breakings,
ordinary shop-breaking—all of London's regular forms of
crime.

"Going to have a hell of a job to watch all that lot," the
Chief Inspector said. He was a tall, thin-faced, black-
moustached man with keen eyes and an inventive mind. He
had thought up a little tool, rather like a cross between a
stapler and a brace and bit, with which to jab the strong shell
pins into the maps; at some spots, where pins were grouped
together in thick forests, this was a job difficult to do without
knocking other pins out.

"I know," Roger said. "As the lists come in from the
Divisions, will you keep 'em recorded?"

"Yes."

"And what have you got to show the shops which have been
robbed?" asked Roger.

The D.I. grinned.

"I'm ready for that one! Red-headed pin with a black dot
instead of a white."

"Thanks," said Roger. "When we catch the beggar behind

all this, I'll let you stick some pins into him." He went out to the accompaniment of broad grins from subordinates of the Map Room, and felt less gloomy. Violet Marsh might not realise it, but she had really been the turning point. He went to his office, checked by telephone that her condition was unchanged, and then talked to Charlie Baker, of Whitechapel.

"Handsome, the Endicott widow hasn't done a thing or seen anyone to make us open our eyes," Baker assured him. "She goes out to the pictures three times a week, and last week she went with some girls to a dance at the Mile End *Palais de Danse*. I had a chap there. No one on your list danced with her, no one talked to her furtively. If she knows anything or anyone, she's being very smart about it."

"Keep watching," Roger said.

"The trouble with you is you forget there are other jobs as well as the one you're working on," grumbled Baker. "Tell you what—you ought to find her a nice new boy friend, someone from one of the other Divisions who wouldn't be recognised round these parts. How's that for a smart idea?"

"Good old Charlie," said Roger, and heard Baker's grunt of satisfaction. "Very smart indeed. I've got the man coming to see me this afternoon."

For that was the moment when he realised that Owen would be wasted on Stone but might be invaluable with Endicott's widow. And almost at the same time he realised how best to shadow Stone.

XI

INTEREST IN RUTH ENDICOTT

"MAY I say this, sir," said Owen, after he had waited for Roger to finish on the telephone, "that I very much appreciate the chance you've given me, and I'll do all I can to justify it."

"May I say this," said Roger, drily, "you wouldn't be standing here if I didn't think you had the qualifications for this particular job. And according to your Superintendent, you've probably got the guts, too." Roger picked up the telephone nearer him, said: "Keep all calls away from me for ten minutes, will you?" and put the receiver down with a bang. "Sit down, Owen—Cyril Owen, isn't it?"

"Yes, sir."

"You don't have to take the job I'm offering you," said Roger, "and I don't want you to take it unless you feel there's a fifty-fifty chance of pulling it off. In the first place, it's bloody dangerous."

"If it's this shop robbery job, I can see that."

"That's the job," said Roger, and looked the young man up and down. Owen was probably in the late twenties; Roger hadn't checked that yet. He was lean, with a rather lantern jaw, and cheeks which sank in a little; his lips were full, if anything a trifle over-full, perhaps faintly Jewish. He had big, very clear, chestnut brown eyes, and reddish hair. Had he been introduced as a University don, Roger would not have been surprised; he had that kind of look about him, but his voice rather spoiled the impression, being a little rough and slightly nasal. "Now here's a question only you can answer. How do you get on with women?"

Owen exclaimed: "With *women*?"

"Do they fall for those big eyes?"

Owen gulped. "I—er—I see what you mean, sir. Well, I've never regarded myself as Don Juan, but I can't complain at being left out in the cold." He coloured. "As a matter of fact, on the whole I think I'm quite a success with the ladies."

"Good. Remember how we found the man Endicott, who murdered Mrs. Stone?"

"Very well, sir."

"See any pictures of his widow?"

"There was a whole page of them in the *Weekly Revel*," Owen said. "She's quite an eyeful. Everywhere, I should imagine!"

"Her husband was probably murdered to stop him from talking, or to make sure he couldn't give the game away. I've never been satisfied that she told me all she could about his friends. I'd like someone to try to find out, but if she knows it's a policeman, she'll dry right up. I've had some. I've also had authority from the Assistant Commissioner to offer you the job of getting to know her, and trying to find out what she knows. If her husband's murderers find out what you're doing, they might cut your throat, and they might cut hers. See what I mean by dangerous?"

"Yes, sir."

"What do you feel about it?"

Owen looked at Roger very steadily for what seemed a long time, then said with great deliberation:

"Can I have a night to think about it, sir?"

"Yes," said Roger at once. "But you aren't to say a word to anyone about the job or anything I've told you about it."

"No, sir."

"Want to know anything else?"

"I don't think that there's anything else I need to know unless I'm going on with the job," said Owen. "I hope you won't think I'm being over-cautious . . ."

"A chance to sleep on it is a good idea," Roger said. "Right —I'll see you in the morning. Go down to the Map Room meanwhile, and ask the D.I. there to let you help sticking in pins on the shop robberies and the shop robbery potential. You'll get a clearer idea of the kind of problem we're up against."

Owen was wise to take the cautious attitude, of course, but

if he was over-cautious on the job, he might miss a big chance if it came. Roger shrugged the disquiet away. He went downstairs and along to that section of the Criminal Investigation Department which was devoted to women officers. Chief Inspector Ethel Winstanley was an old friend of his, and it didn't surprise him that as soon as he entered, she rang the bell for tea; and when tea was on the desk, with two fragile bone china cups, she said:

"Milk, no sugar, and you want someone to find out where Jim Stone goes, don't you?"

"Bellew been bellowing?" Roger inquired.

"Loud enough," answered Ethel Winstanley. She was a stocky, square-shouldered woman who had come into prominence during the Cyprus troubles when she had been out in the island to help the military police, for she had a good knowledge of Greek and of Turkish. No one knew quite what strings she had pulled to get into the Metropolitan Police, but once in, her career had been almost sensational. "I think I've just the girl for you, Superintendent, and I've been thinking about the best way for her to go about it."

Roger sipped his tea.

"This gets better and better," he said. "Did anyone happen to mention the possibility of flick knives and blunt instruments?"

"I think the girl I have in mind should pose as a sob sister on one of the lesser-known women's magazines," said Ethel, without answering the question. "I can fix it with the *Home Talk* editor, and I'm pretty sure this man Stone will simply say no when she first asks him for a heart-throb story. But if he sees her following him about, he won't be too surprised."

Roger took a long drink of his tea, put the cup down, and said:

"She's my girl, on one condition."

"What's that?"

"Her job is to watch Stone, and tell us where he disappears to, to make a complete log of his movements. Her job is not to attempt to find the murderer of Endicott or Gantry."

"She's a sensible girl and she won't want her throat cut,"

Ethel Winstanley said. "I don't know whether you've met her before. I'm thinking of Detective Sergeant Dawson."

"I know her," Roger said. "The Plain Jane who helped with that gold smuggling job last year. Is she handy?"

"I can send for her."

"I want to read her the riot act on what she can and can't do," Roger said. "But I'll have another cup of tea, first." He finished the tea, and a few minutes afterwards Detective Sergeant Dawson was summoned. He had called her Plain Jane, and there was a lot of justification for it; no one would ever call her attractive insofar as attractiveness meant beauty, but she had quite a figure, nice legs, very nice hands, and if her nose was a bit lumpy and her mouth too full and plummy, there was intelligence and humour in her clear blue eyes.

Roger read his riot act.

"I will follow your instructions closely, sir," promised Bella Dawson. "If there is the slightest indication of physical danger, I shall send for male help."

Her eyes weren't actually twinkling.

Ethel Winstanley's were.

· · · · · ·

On the following morning, a little after ten o'clock, James Stone returned to the shop in Kemp Road, Clapham. He had not given Mrs. Klein or Gwen, the assistant, any warning, and Gwen was there alone, making up orders, her cluster of auburn curls quite lovely as she bent over her order book; she was a little short-sighted. She looked up quickly as the door opened, started, and said:

"Mr. Stone!"

"Hallo, Gwen," Stone said. "Is Mrs. Klein in?"

"She isn't this morning, as a matter of fact," said Gwen, "she's gone to get her hair done."

"She's done *what*?"

"She's gone to get her hair done, it was ever so greasy, and I'm quite all right——"

Stone said harshly: "I don't want either of you to be alone in this shop again—ever. If I'm not here, get a neighbour, or hire someone else, but don't stay here alone. Understand that?"

"I—I'm perfectly all right, Mr. Stone," Gwen protested.

He stared at her, and he thought: "That's what Mabel believed." He was always thinking about Mabel, blaming himself for ever leaving her alone, and hating himself for what he had allowed to happen to her and to the unborn child. There were so many things he wished he had done during their marriage, the many things she would have liked, the places she would have visited; but he had always been so careful, so anxious to save. Now he had plenty of money, all the money he could want, and no one to share it with, and the feeling that in a way he had robbed Mabel.

It hurt to think of her.

It had been like a savage torture in the early days, when he had talked to West, fighting for self control, somehow making it appear as if he were taking the loss well, actually aflame with anger and hatred. Then West had said something which had stung him into saying that he would hunt the murderer down, and that had eased his tension and his agony. Nothing else did. He could not talk to his mother, to Gwen, or to anyone; but he could make promises to Mabel almost as if she were alive.

"I'll make them pay for it, Mab."

"Don't worry, pet, I'll kill them for killing you."

"I'll kill the devils, Mab."

After the discovery of the murderer's body, he had been stunned, and for a few hours the hurt of Mabel's loss had been greater than ever, but then his thoughts had carried him to a different mood; a newspaper, he did not remember which one, had first suggested that Endicott had been murdered to stop him from talking, and implied that there was a gang involved —a gang of men organised to go round to rob shopkeepers, to attack and to murder defenceless women.

And the police did *nothing*.

Stone felt no personal animosity towards West; in fact he rather liked West. But he also sensed that there was nothing that the Yard man could do to help him. As he had told West, he had spent days at the local library looking up back copies of newspapers, and had been amazed and appalled by the number of attacks on shopkeepers which were reported and the few which seemed to be solved by the police. The determination to search for the murderer of Endicott, and so for the real murderer of Mabel, had come slowly, yet once he had accepted the need, it seemed a normal, natural objective. It did not matter what it cost, he must find the man who had killed Endicott. He could spend everything he had, all *Mabel's* money, on seeking vengeance.

He had seen his mother only once since the funeral, and had a bitter quarrel because she had obviously seen Mabel's death as a good thing for him; she had never liked Mabel, and never understood his love for her.

The newspapers helped in his task, chiefly the *Globe*, the paper which had employed the clever artist. The *Globe* had told the story of Endicott's death "through the eyes of his lonely widow" and he had read that closely and then read everything he could find about this woman, Ruth Endicott. By far the biggest and most informative article had been in a popular weekly magazine, the *Home Talk*. That had concentrated on her face, and she was quite nice looking, and on her figure; it had shown pictures of her in bathing suits, bikinis, almost in nothing at all. The captions had meant little, but reading between the lines Stone had come to one conclusion.

Endicott's widow must know who had employed her husband, and therefore who had killed him.

So Stone had set out to get to know Ruth Endicott, so that he could learn everything she could tell him. He knew exactly what he had to do, and he also understood the dangers. If those employers knew that he was interested in her, then they were quite ruthless enough to kill her as they had her husband; or to kill him. It had to be something very clever, something which no one would suspect; he had to make the woman's acquaintance soon, but quite naturally.

Then he thought: "I wonder where she shops?"

One of his tasks had been to go to the neighbourhood where she lived—that sordid, squalid part of the East End—without being recognised, for his photograph had been in all the news-papers. The answer to that had come simply and, like the answer to everything else, quite logically. He must disguise himself. The simple way was to wear a beard. No one was committing a crime by doing that. He could get one from a theatrical make-up place, what did they call them?—theatrical costumiers. He could have one fitted, could find out how it was done, could pretend that he was going to take part in some amateur theatricals. They wouldn't care what he was going to do with the beard, all they would want was the sale.

It had cost ten guineas. When he fitted it on, it altered his appearance completely, and there was no risk of anyone re-cognising him unless they knew him well. With it, he could go where he liked in the Whitechapel district, and the first time he went there—without saying a word to anyone—he concentrated on finding out where Ruth Endicott shopped, especially where she bought her groceries and oddment shopping.

It did not take him long to find out that she patronised two places.

Once he knew that, the next step was quite logical and quite natural; he had to buy one of the shops.

XII

NEW OWNER

THE shop near the Whitechapel Road was the larger, much better stocked, a much better business proposition, but it would need a lot of capital, and at least five assistants. In any case, the Cockell shop group was interested, and it was ideal for conversion to a supermarket. The other shop, nearer Brasher's Row, was much more the kind of business which Stone hoped to get; he would be able to buy it, stock and goodwill together, for no more than three thousand pounds, and the elderly man and woman who kept it would probably think themselves lucky to get as much. One of the daughters of the old couple came over to the shop once or twice a week, to let her parents go out for a few hours; otherwise, they were tied to the place day in and day out.

Having discovered the shop, Stone was desperately eager to get possession, but with a systematic and logical approach which had always characterised him, he knew that he must go about it carefully, so that no one could have the slightest idea of what he was doing. That was why he just disappeared from time to time; if Mrs. Klein or Gwen had known where he was going it would be dangerous, for the police would find out; if he lied to them, the lie might be discovered; if he went off without a word and came back when he wanted to, they would come to accept this, and they would not have him questioned.

On the first of his disappearances, he had discovered the addresses of the two shops and also discovered a business Transfer Agency in Aldgate which specialised in the sale of small shops. Wearing his beard, he went there and said that he was looking for premises in a certain area, within the two to four thousand pounds price range, inclusive of goodwill; he "explained" that he had spent his childhood in the district, and had always wanted to come back. Myerson, the youthful-looking Jew who talked to him, was completely uninterested in his reasons; the Jew was bright, alert, rather quick-speaking, a man who knew practically every shop in the East End of London, and who realised quite well that from time to time the police watched him because he was suspected of dealing in stolen goods. He was completely free from serious suspicion, completely innocent of crime, and in fact a contented and honest man who acted as unofficial moneylender in the district at reasonable rates of interest.

Myerson had an application form filled in on which the would-be buyer gave his name as Simpson, Joseph Simpson; and he promised not only to arrange a view of all shops now on sale, but to find out if others would be suitable. When Joseph Simpson said that he was moving about a lot, and would come and see him occasionally, while letters could be addressed at a collecting office in Battersea, the Jew asked no questions. This client had the finance, he knew what he wanted; it was no business of his, Myerson's, where he had obtained the money.

None of the shops which Simpson saw on his first trip with Myerson was what he wanted, but on the second visit, Myerson greeted him effusively.

"I have just the business you want, Mr. Simpson, the very one! An old couple own it, they are not very hard-working people, they have very little capital, so it has gone down, down, down. And it is not the right position for a supermarket. Mind you, it can become a very good business, very good indeed. Personal service, that is what it needs, personal service. And this old couple, they have a country cottage, ready and waiting for them, a customer for the shop could not find the money, after all, and they have the cottage ready. So they will sell to you for——" Myerson's deepset eyes were very thoughtful, as if he were trying to calculate the highest figure that Simpson would go to. "For fifteen hundred pounds, yes, and also the property itself for fifteen hundred pounds more. You have everything—freehold property, business, stock, goodwill, all for three thousand pounds. Isn't that what you want?"

"It might be," Simpson said. "Where is it?"

"Mr. Simpson, my car is outside, this very minute we can

go and show you these premises, and although I warn you they
need decoration, they need some repair, there is no better
business position in all of the East End of London. Come,
please!" Myerson slapped on a Homburg hat that was a
little too large for him; it pressed his large ears down. Then
he led the way, flatfooted, out to a Hillman Minx, weaved
through Aldgate's thick traffic, and brought his client to the
shop where Mrs. Endicott did much of her shopping.

Stone, *alias* Simpson, hummed and hawed and finally
offered two thousand five hundred pounds; they split the
difference.

"When can I take over?" he demanded.

"In a week's time, Mr. Simpson, or two weeks—just as soon
as you wish it."

"Let's make it in a week's time," said Simpson-Stone.

. . . . . .

His first job was to give an order to a local painter and de-
corator to paint the front of the shop, and a signwriter to
write: *Jos. Simpson*. He was tempted to have the paint white
on red, but did not in case someone else realised how much
like the shop in Kemp Road it was. He moved in at the week-
end, and spent all of Sunday turning out the stock rooms at the
back, getting some kind of order out of the chaos, studying
the figures, especially the mass of bad debts. He hoped to find
that Mrs. Endicott was one who owed money, but her account
was always paid up weekly; however, she always came in
several times a week.

. . . . . .

One of the peculiar facts about the disappearance of Jim
Stone from Clapham was that he did not realise that he was
being watched by the "woman reporter" from some weekly
gossip paper. She had asked him for an interview, he had
refused flatly, and the second time, he had been rude to her.
He had noticed her about several times since then, but gave
her very little thought. He was in fact looking out for a plain-
clothes detective, who he knew was keeping an eye open for

him. When the man failed to appear for three days in a row, Stone hoped that the police had given up, but was still very careful. He had planned his actions thoroughly, and knew exactly what he meant to do.

He woke up on the Saturday morning, one of the busy mornings, said that he was going to get the van out, went to the yard—and simply disappeared.

Detective Sergeant Bella Dawson had a room in a house nearly opposite this yard, and she was up and dressed, half expecting him to go out in the van. She went downstairs to get her motor-scooter out of the backyard. When she reached the street she heard the grocery van's engine warming up. She was over-tired and a little careless, because on the previous occasions when Stone had disappeared, he had not taken the van. He drove out of the alleyway which led to the shop's backyard, as she reached the corner of Kemp Road and Middleton Street. He went on towards the High Street and the Common, and she followed. So did another motor-scooter, a moped and a small car; there was nothing at all unusual in such a stream of traffic.

A combination of traffic lights, a greedy motorist who cut her off, and astuteness on the part of Stone, gave Bella Dawson her unhappiest morning for a long time. She saw the van pull round a corner near a biscuit wholesalers, felt quite satisfied that Stone was getting supplies, followed leisurely and parked some way along the street where the van was parked, and waited for him to show up again.

He didn't appear.

.   .   .   .   .

"I know what he did, Mr. West—he just walked away from the van and left it parked. I checked as closely as I could, but I can't be even sure which way he went. I'm desperately sorry."

"It can't be helped," said Roger. "He'll probably be back in a few days and you can have another go."

He dismissed Bella Dawson, resisted the temptation to tell himself that in the same circumstances a male officer wouldn't have been fooled, and drafted a general call for news of Stone, making it clear that this was for police stations only; he simply wanted information.

Roger was disgruntled and still uneasy; the whole case seemed to be dogged by this kind of "bad luck". And when a week passed, and there was still no sign of Stone, no message, no news of any kind, he began to think that they had lost the man for good.

He wondered whether Cyril Owen was going to box up his side of the job, like Bella Dawson.

.   .   .   .   .   .

Once he had accepted the commission to work on the Shop Robberies case, Detective Constable Cyril Owen settled down to work out the details and to decide exactly how he was to to go about the job. He did not know it, but he had a lot in common with Stone, particularly the logical mind and the ability to take a situation calmly. His one lapse with West had taught him the folly of speaking on impulse, and he was determined not to make that kind of mistake again.

His first task had been to find a reasonable explanation of why he should move to the Brasher's Row area, and he hit on a similar idea to Stone's, although there were some important differences. The one thing Owen knew plenty about was bicycles. The internal combustion engine didn't greatly interest him, and he regarded mo-peds, or power-assisted cycles, as the refuge of the effete; but he could take a bicycle to pieces lovingly, and reassemble it so that it was as good as new.

In the Whitechapel Road was a big cycle shop, which dealt in second-hand machines. At one time this had been owned by a man who had sold more stolen bicycles than anyone else in London, but it was now owned by Mr. and Mrs. Walsh, a young couple who were as honest as Myerson, and who had only one trouble; lack of staff. They both worked late into the evening and at most week-ends, and the only help they got was from unreliables.

Regularly the Walsh's advertised for a cycle mechanic, and when they had a call from a youthful man wearing a windcheater and green plus-fours, a little freakish in this day and age, they were puzzled. Certainly he wasn't like any of the other applicants. He gave his name as Orde, Cyril Orde, and said simply that he loved "messing about with bikes". He had never been an official mechanic before, but if they would care to give him a week's trial, say, they would have some idea whether he was any good. He was fed up with his present job, and provided he earned enough to live on, that was all he wanted. And—could they recommend a place where he could rent a room? He didn't mind getting his own food.

The room the Walsh's recommended was not in Brasher's Row, but in a street leading to it. On his way to his room, Owen had to pass a corner grocery shop, which was being re-painted during his first week-end in the district. Owen gave it no thought, except to note that it was the kind of shop which had been raided so often. There seemed little risk of a shop in this neighbourhood being on the danger list, dog didn't eat dog. Owen actually passed the bearded owner of the shop, presumably the Jos. Simpson of the fascia board, but did not suspect his real identity.

Owen's next job was to find a way of getting to know Ruth Endicott, and it wasn't difficult to lead up to the subject of Ruth at the shop, where lanky, prematurely bald Walsh immediately swallowed the bait.

"Yes, that chap Endicott lived near here, in Brasher's Row as a matter of fact. He was a proper swine, used to beat his wife black and blue, no one could ever understand why she put up with it. Nice girl, Ruth is. My wife used to go to school with her. You never know when she might pop in, she bought a machine from us a few months ago, comes in to have it oiled and cleaned. She never did like getting her hands dirty."

"If she didn't like work, perhaps that's what her husband didn't like," remarked Owen, lightly—and realised at once that the flippancy did not go down too well. It had been flippancy which had annoyed Superintendent West, he would have to check all such impulses. As the situation was, he had worked into the right position nicely, and if he played his cards well he ought to be taking Ruth Endicott out within a

week or two. He had underrated himself to West, thinking
modesty wise; the truth was, most girls found it easy to like
Cyril Owen.

.   .   .   .   .

During the period that Stone and Owen were angling for
position, and the week in which they got settled and were
poised to start work on the widow, who had not the slightest
idea of their interest, Roger West put the finishing touches to
the campaign against the Shop Robberies.

Each Division had now supplied the details required. The
maps in the Map Room were smothered with the red-headed
pins with white and black dots to distinguish between shops
which had been robbed, and shops which might be. More-
over, all the police forces in the country, as well as the Divisions, had made arrangements to report shop robberies to
Roger by teletype. On the wall of his own office he had a
sketch map of England and Wales, with a supply of the Map
Room's pins. He had a Chief Inspector, two detective sergeants and three detective officers working on the job, sifting
all reports, and sending through any which they thought
wanted his personal attention.

Any similarities in the way shops were raided, all similarities in the kinds of goods stolen, and everything the local
police discovered, were carefully noted. In the London
Divisions, Roger had managed to arrange a system by which
every shop which might be raided was passed by a policeman
on duty at least once an hour. It meant that other places were
watched very sketchily, and had obvious dangers, but he
persuaded his superiors to take that chance. One thing became
apparent; only the "little man's" shop was raided. No supermarkets were affected, even when one was within a few hundred yards of a neighbourhood shop.

It was on a day two months after Mrs. Stone's murder that
an eruption came.

XIII

ERUPTION

Roger's telephone bell rang, about five o'clock that Monday afternoon, and it was Bellew; an excited and unusually breathless Bellew.

"Handsome, we've had five shop raids this afternoon—five, in the space of half an hour, all at different parts of the manor."

"Catch anyone?" demanded Roger.

"Two of our chaps have been knocked about, and they've got good descriptions," Bellew said. "But the answer is no—we didn't catch anyone. Handsome——"

He broke off.

"Yes?"

"There were two men involved in each raid—one to do the job, one on a motor-scooter round the corner. The raider rushed out and got on the pillion and off they went. You remember that motor-scooter which Gantry used?"

"I remember," Roger said, and as he spoke, the door of the office opened and almost at the same instant, the other telephone bell rang. "Let me have details as soon as you can, Jack, will you? My other phone's ringing." He rang off; a middle-aged Detective Sergeant in the doorway had a glint of excitement in his eyes, a rare thing. Roger lifted the receiver of the telephone, said: "Half a minute," and looked at the plain-clothes man. "What's eating you, Sam?"

"There's a hell of a do out at Putney, and plenty of trouble at Battersea. Nine shops have been raided in all."

"Anyone caught?"

"Not yet. Couple of our chaps copped a packet, and——"

"The raiders got off on motor-scooters," Roger finished for him. "Just a minute." He put the other receiver to his ear more tightly, gripping it very firmly, and said into it: "West here, what's on?"

"Information Room here, sir," said the man at the other end of the line. "There are reports of shop raids coming in from all over South-west London."

"Only South-west London?"

"Yes, so far?"

"How many?"

"I've got up to twenty-one, sir."

"Keep counting and advise me every fifteen minutes," Roger said, and then raised his voice: "Don't go!" He picked up a pencil, hesitated, and then said: "What time were these raids?"

"I've got the times they were reported, that's all."

"Get the times of the raids themselves."

"Right, sir."

Roger rang off, his heart thumping as he made notes on a pad in front of him, writing swiftly but with great deliberation. "Looks like real trouble, Sam," he remarked. "Take this note along to the Commander. If he's not in, take it to the Assistant Commissioner. It's an official request to put all Divisions and the Yard on an overtime basis tonight and to-morrow."

"I'll get busy," Sam promised.

There was a frightening significance in what Roger had been told, something which would give the Yard their biggest headache for a long, long time. Until now, the raids had mostly been carried out sporadically, perhaps as many as four or five in the same evening, but nothing to suggest that a big force of raiders was involved. The present score was in the twenties, and might rise to twice that number. Roger tried to picture the situation in which forty men might start out. Forty? There were two men on each job, so if forty shops had been raided, eighty men had been involved.

He said: "It can't happen."

His telephone bell rang.

"Information here," said the man who had called him a few minutes ago. "The total score now is thirty-three, but new reports have stopped coming in."

"Well, that's a relief," Roger said. "Any times in yet?"

"They all started about five o'clock—that is, all I've been able to check yet."

"Yes," said Roger. "What Division?"

He made notes as the answers came, looking at the wall map from time to time, and when he rang off he stood up and went to the map, then began to shade several adjacent Divisions with pencil. He was doing this when the elderly Detective Sergeant came in.

"The Commander was with the A.C., sir. They said they'd be in touch with you very soon."

"Thanks."

"What's that?" asked the sergeant, and came forward. Then he went on: "My God, do you see what I see?"

"Four Divisions affected, each of them next to another affected one," Roger said. "And that tells a story, doesn't it, Sam? The raiders made sure one Division couldn't rush help to another. At five o'clock the bridges are so busy that cross-river progress would be hopelessly slow." He broke off, as there was a brisk tap at the door, and the door opened before he could call "come in". The big, broad, neatly dressed figure of Hardy, the Commander C.I.D., appeared in the doorway. Hardy's grey hair was smoothed down, his rather deep-set eyes had, as always, a rather worried look. He had a strong, quite handsome face but rather thin lips.

"Come in, sir," Roger said.

"I'm not staying," said Hardy. "There's a conference in the Public Prosecutor's Office over the Miden case, but I wanted you to know that I've signed the overtime orders."

"Thanks."

"Think we ought to stop leave?" asked Hardy.

"That's going to be tough, in the middle of August," Roger said. "I'd wait until we see just what turns up."

"I'll leave it to you, then. How many reported raids to date?"

"Thirty-three."

"Sixty-six men," Hardy remarked. He smoothed one hand over his flat hair, and gave a faint, unamused smile. "Well, at least you don't take a smug satisfaction out of saying

'I told you so'. If big stores suffer we're going to be under pressure."

"Look after the big boys, and hang the little man," Roger said sardonically.

"I'm just looking ahead," Hardy said. "If anything else of importance comes in, let me know before I leave. I'll be in my office until seven o'clock."

"I'll let you know," Roger promised.

He watched the Commander go out, as old Sam, who had seemed to merge with the wall while the senior officer was present, came forward again. The telephone kept silent, yet there was a constant air of expectancy.

"See how they start to worry when big interests are hit in their pockets, don't you? Wonder Cockell shops haven't started to squeal too. Eight of their stores were raided."

"They'll start squealing," Roger said, "and they're very vulnerable if they employ men like Gantry. Might be a good idea to talk to them before they call us. Find out who their managing director is, will you?"

"Right," said the sergeant. "Those eight supermarkets lost nearly a thousand quid apiece, and there are twenty-five jobs of at least a couple of hundred quid each. It's a hell of a lot of money."

"We need details of everything stolen, and we want immediate action on the Wholesaler and Warehouse emergency system," Roger said, "I'll draft a note for the teleprinter. You get it out, will you?"

"Pronto."

Roger pulled the pad closer to him, and after a moment's pause, wrote quickly:

"All thirty-three shop raids today evidently carefully timed and cleverly planned. Stop. No total figures yet but substantial stocks of cigarettes already reported stolen. Stop. Please refer my Memo. dated July 10th and arrange for watch on all tobacco warehouses and wholesalers for deliveries this evening or through the night.

R. West. Superintendent."

He handed this to the sergeant as his telephone bell rang again. It wasn't yet six o'clock, so in an hour, the whole situation had changed completely. In the background was a driving anxiety, the knowledge that the people behind this could lay on sixty-six people to work at the same time, and could plan and time it all so that the raids went off without a hitch.

So far, there was no report that anyone had been caught; it was almost impossible to believe that every one of the sixty-six people could get away, but Roger had to remember that each attack had been complete in itself, and thoroughly prepared.

The caller was Appleby.

"Having a n-nice t-time?" the pathologist inquired.

"How much have you heard?"

"I've just come from the A.C.'s office," said Appleby. "He's busy wishing he'd l-l-listened to you before. Going t-t-to have any luck?"

"It doesn't look like it yet."

"Can I help?"

"I'll call you if you can."

"Like me to call Janet and t-t-tell her you'll be late?"

"Will you?" asked Roger, and heard Appleby chuckle. He rang off, glad that there was no need to tell Janet himself that he wouldn't be home until midnight; he would be lucky to get home at all.

One problem was how to visit all the places where the raids had taken place; it would take him days. But he had an even greater problem.

He had been convinced all along that some of the robberies were connected, but it hadn't dawned on him that anything like so many men would be involved. He certainly hadn't anticipated raids on anything like this scale, and it might be only the beginning. The effect had been cumulative, and the next obvious step for an organisation as strong as this would be to raid places where there was more loot—banks, post offices and wages offices, for instance. The more he contemplated this the more dangerous the possibilities threatened to be.

Then the door opened with a rush, and the Detective
Sergeant came in, his eyes glowing.

"We caught two of them, sir. Over at Battersea."

.   .   .   .   .

Just before five o'clock that afternoon, a youthful police
constable in the Battersea Division, a man named O'Hara, had
been walking along Park Street, which led to Battersea Park
through a colony of flats and small houses. There was very
little trouble for the police in this area, and most of what there
was came when the Battersea Fun Fair was open, and some of
the youngsters lost their heads or had too much to drink.

O'Hara, a married man with three school-age children, was
thinking about the shop robberies, and in fact was quickening
his pace so that he could see the four shops in his area at least
once an hour. There were times when he thought that it was
a waste of time; that if any trouble came, it could be reported
very quickly and the police could be there within a few
minutes. Then he laughed at himself, realising that he was
supposed to be preventing crime, not solving it. He had not a
great deal of imagination, but where his mind worked it worked
well.

He saw the two men turn round a corner on a motor-
scooter.

A man and a girl on one of the noisy little machines wasn't
unusual, and two girls was quite usual, but two men—that
was worthy of notice. These chaps were smallish, too, and
they handled the machine like experts. It had bright blue
cellulose and a big plastic windshield, and had specially fitted
carriers which could hold a lot of luggage. O'Hara turned and
watched it—and saw that the pillion passenger was looking at
him the sly way that men up to no good often look at the police.
He went on slowly, until the motor-scooter turned the corner;
next time he glanced round, it was out of sight, but he could
hear its popping engine.

It stopped.

By then, O'Hara had recalled the *Police Gazette* report
about the man Gantry, and the fact that he had gone to the

raid on Mrs. Marsh on a motor-scooter. O'Hara spun round.
The engine was still silent. A cyclist turned into the street,
an insurance agent whom he knew slightly, and who lived just
round the next corner. He hurried towards the man, waving;
and the cyclist swerved towards him.

"Call my Station, say I think I'll need help at the corner of
Atholl Street and Blair Road," he ordered. "Just tell them
that, and——" He broke off, realising that this man's bicycle
would be invaluable. "Let me have your bike," he said
urgently. "You run with that message."

The insurance agent pushed the machine towards him.

"Are you sure——" he began.

"Just send that message!" O'Hara ordered. He forked the
machine and pedalled furiously towards the corner, and round
it. He saw the motor-scooter outside the shop on the corner;
the rider was still astride it, but the pillion-rider wasn't there.
The rider looked over his shoulder, and almost at once he blew
the horn of the scooter three times; the horn had a distinctive
high-pitched note. O'Hara knew exactly what to do as he
raced towards the scooter, and as the pillion rider came running out of the shop, carrying a sack. The luggage carriers
were open. O'Hara was within a few yards of them both when
he saw a bottle in one man's hand, raised to throw. Instead
of jumping off his machine and rushing at them, O'Hara leapt
off on the side away from them—and gave the bicycle a
violent shove, so that it hurtled towards the motor-scooter.

It was the one move which the two men hadn't anticipated.

XIV

HERO O'HARA

O'HARA landed on both feet, but nearly lost his balance. As he weaved about, he saw the front wheel of the borrowed bicycle bang into the side of the motor-scooter, and the pedals scraped along the machine, screeching. The bottle of fruit cordial crashed on the pavement. A pedal caught the ankle of the rider, who reared up with pain. The pillion passenger nearly fell off, but held on. As O'Hara steadied, he saw the man flash his right hand to his trousers pocket.

A flick knife blade spat out, catching the light.

The motor-scooter fell with a crash, pinning the rider's leg beneath it. Out of the corner of his eyes O'Hara saw the man trying desperately to free himself; he also saw the man with the knife half crouching, ready for him, the narrow pointed blade quite capable of causing death at a single thrust. Two girls turned the corner, and one of them cried out: "*Look, Elsie!*" The rider was still struggling to get out from under the machine.

O'Hara called: "Drop that knife!"

The man with the knife didn't speak, just stood crouching for a split second, and the rider pulled himself free. O'Hara snatched out his truncheon, and leapt forward. One of the girls screamed. The man with the knife ducked and came in, to deliver a vicious upwards thrust with his killer weapon, which was exactly what O'Hara had expected. He kicked at the man's wrist, caught the knife and sent it flying upwards into the air in a shimmering arc. Then he brought his truncheon down on top of the raider's head. He heard the man grunt as he fell, side-stepped his falling body, and heard the girl scream:

"*Look out!*"

He swung round towards the rider of the scooter, who was coming at him with a knife. O'Hara stood motionless for a moment, until it looked as if the man couldn't fail to stab him; then he swayed to one side, and swung a powerful blow with the truncheon, catching his second assailant on the side of the head. The timing of the blow was so perfect that it sent the man staggering forward, partly under his own momentum; then he slipped off the kerb and pitched down. As the knife flew from his hand and skidded along the road, O'Hara took three long strides and banged him on the nape of the neck, a comparatively gentle but effective truncheon blow.

He straightened up, made sure that his first victim was still unconscious, tucked his truncheon away, and saw that in addition to the two girls, a woman with a pram, an elderly man and two middle-aged men had gathered and were staring at him as if bewildered.

"Keep an eye on these two, will you?" he asked the crowd in general. "I'd better see if everything's all right in the shop."

He entered the shop, and saw the till wide open, money strewn about the floor and on the counter, a frightened middle-aged woman standing in a doorway at the back of the shop, with a broom in her hand, as if ready to fight the raiders if they came back. A scared-looking boy in his early teens stood behind the cheese counter, holding a bottle of orange squash. O'Hara's first temptation was to grin. Instead, he said:

"It's all right, Mrs. Dixon, nothing more to worry about. Did they take anything?"

"I don't think he had any time to," said the woman, breathlessly. "I thought—I thought he was going to kill you, I did really."

"Take more than a sneak thief to do that," boomed O'Hara, and then heard a car coming fast along the street. "Stay where you are, and there'll be nothing to worry about." He went outside, to see a car from Divisional Headquarters pulling up, and for the first time felt that he could relax. Then he saw something dark sticking out of the pocket of the man he had first knocked out. He bent down, picked it up, and found that it was a triangular piece of plastic, with slits cut out for the eyes; a simple form of mask.

A uniformed sergeant was getting out of the car.

"And they told us you needed help," he scoffed.

.   .   .   .   .   .

Roger looked at the two prisoners, small, sallow, bleary-eyed men, one of whom had been unconscious for twenty-five minutes. The bruises on their heads were indications of the power of Constable O'Hara's blows. Proud O'Hara was next door, making out his report; the two prisoners were in the charge room of the Battersea Divisional Station, and two local C.I.D. men were with Roger. The prisoners had been searched and the contents of their pockets bagged, labelled and set aside. The pillion rider's sack was there, too, and it was obvious that this was used to carry the loot out of the shop; the carriers of the motor-scooter could hold a lot of cigarettes and small goods.

"Now let's have it straight," Roger said. "Who do you work for?"

One of the men said sneering: "We're self-employed, that's what we are."

"If you keep that up you'll get yourselves into worse trouble than you are now," Roger said. "Who's your employer?"

"*He's* my employer," one man said, pointing to the second man.

"He's mine, mister," said the second man, pointing to the first.

"What they want is another ten minutes with O'Hara, he'd knock some sense into them," a local man growled.

"He might," Roger said. "If they don't knock some sense into themselves the judge soon will. What's the maximum sentence for robbery with violence?"

"Ten years," the local C.I.D. man answered.

"You won't get us for ten years," said the smaller of the two.

Roger eyed them keenly and thoughtfully, and with the sense of frustration which was with him so much in this job. These men would not give anything away. What they said had been carefully prepared, and probably carefully rehearsed. They knew perfectly well that the police realised that this was one of a series of raids, but could insist that it had been an isolated one, thought up for themselves. They weren't going to be easy to break down. One was probably of Italian extraction, but both spoke the Cockney of the native East Ender. They were thin-faced, sneeringly insolent, very sure of themselves.

"I want scrapings from their nails, and have them wash their hands in clean, warm water without a detergent," Roger ordered. "Put the dirty water in a bottle and let me have it with the nail scrapings, will you. Then we'll have 'em up with the others in the morning."

The taller of the two drew in a sharp breath. The Italian began: "What oth——?" and then broke off. Was he really surprised that there were others, or because he thought that the police had made other arrests?

Roger said: "You didn't think you were the only two to get caught in that raid, did you?"

The taller man said: "I dunno what you're talking about."

But he wasn't so sure of himself, and if the police could put half a dozen of the raiders up in the dock next morning it might make one prisoner break down. Roger didn't speak again, and the prisoners were taken out and down to the cells. He turned to the Inspector in charge, and said:

"Mind if I have a word with O'Hara?"

"Glad if you do," said the C.I. "He always did love a fight; it must be the Irish in him." He sent for the constable, who came in briskly: a big man with gingerish hair, clear blue eyes, and massive shoulders.

"O'Hara, this is Chief Superintendent West," said the C.I.

"It's a real pleasure to meet such a famous officer," said O'Hara warmly.

Roger grinned.

"So you kissed the Blarney stone too." After a pause, while all the others smiled dutifully, he went on: "This makes you quite a hero, O'Hara."

"Who, me, sir? I was only doing me duty, and when I saw the two varmints I said to meself, I said, it's ten to one in pints of Guinness that they're carrying knives, and if they're carrying knives then it's up to me to use me truncheon. So use it I did, with a vengeance. But I'm no hero, Mr. West. I could eat a dozen little shrimps of that size and be ready for my breakfast afterwards. Which reminds me, sir," he went on to the Chief Inspector, "my wife was asking me if I could have half a day off on Saturday, 'tis the birthday of one of me daughters."

Roger grinned.

"I think we can manage it," the local Inspector said drily.

"It's very good of you indeed," said O'Hara. "I've written the whole story in me report, sir."

"I'll check it," Roger said. "What made you suspect them?"

"That I couldn't rightly say," declared O'Hara. "It was a combination of circumstances, as you might say. They looked top heavy on the scooter, and they'd got the carrier bags. I glanced round at them and one of them looked round at me, sly like. Then when they'd turned the corner there was a sudden silence, which meant they'd stopped the engine, and I knew there was Mrs. Dixon and her son alone in that shop on the corner. You can say that you caught the two devils yourself, Mr. West. If you hadn't made all of us policemen so aware of the danger to shopkeepers, I wouldn't have given it a second thought."

Roger was still chuckling when he left the police station, with the water in which the men had washed, and the scrapings from their finger-nails; but he sobered down as he drove back to the Yard, with the radio on. No more arrests had been made, but detailed reports were coming in from all South West London. There were now thirty-six known robberies; the total proceeds of the haul were in the neighbourhood of eight thousand pounds in cash, and four thousand in cigarettes and tobacco. Reports were all very similar, but a variety of vehicles from motor-scooters to motor-cycles, little cars and stolen cars, had been used; some raids had been carried out by men on bicycles. Each raider had carried a canvas sack, to hold his loot, and the containers on the captured scooter were large enough to hold fifty or more packs of 100 cigarettes, in tens or twenties. Four men and two women had been injured, none of them seriously.

"There's only one thing common to each raid," Sergeant Sam Ede told him when he got back to the office.

"What's that, Sam?"

"They all wore masks."

"So the radio told me. Same kind of masks?"

"No such luck. Some wore scarves, some wore handkerchiefs, some harlequin masks," the sergeant reported. "But it makes a big change, doesn't it? They didn't intend to be recognised easily. Not like the one who killed Mrs. Stone."

Roger said: "No. That wasn't true to form."

He sent the washing water and nail scrapings to the laboratory for analysis, then took out the articles found in the pockets of the two prisoners. He had arranged for the Yard's fingerprint experts to check them all, but first wanted to take a good look. The men had refused to give their names, and there might be a clue to their identity.

He noticed a lobster claw.

There was nothing remarkable about it, except that it was an unusual thing to find in a man's pocket—rather as if, instead of carrying a rabbit's paw for luck, this man had carried the claw. Roger turned it over with the end of a pencil. There it was, pink and white, with the serrated edge which could give quite a nip. It was polished and apparently had been in the man's pocket for a long time. It struck a chord in his memory, and he looked up at Sam.

"Seen anything like that before, Sam?"

"Don't like shellfish myself, but my old woman's daft on lobster. Likes it served with a cheese sauce, too—she says it's lovely."

"Get the records on Gantry and Endicott, will you?" said Roger. "I want to know what they had in their pockets." He was looking at the contents of the pockets of the second prisoner, and frowning.

Among these was a very small, fan-shaped shell; he wasn't sure what shellfish it came from. It was yellowish in colour, very delicate, and about the size of a shilling. It was the kind of thing one might pick up at the sea-shore and put in one's pocket as a souvenir; the boys had been very fond of doing that when they were young. Sam had gone out, and Roger was alone for ten minutes, trying to remember what had been in the pockets of the two murdered men, wondering why these shells rang a bell in his mind.

Sam came in with the list.

"Funny thing here, Mr. West."

"What's that, Sam?"

"Endicott didn't have anything like it on him, but Gantry did—he carried a winkle shell. A plain ordinary winkle, like you pick up in thousands at Southend when the tide's out, but—what's that one, sir?"

"Just another shell," Roger said. "We might be on to something here, if it isn't just coincidence. Sam, I'm going to make a round of the four Divisions where they had trouble. Tell the night man to contact me at them, will you?"

"Going shell collecting?"

"I wouldn't be surprised," Roger said. "What about those laboratory reports?"

"Just came in," Sam said. "One man's been handling a lot of bacon, lately. The other had vegetable dirt on his hands and fingers—as if he worked in a greengrocer's shop."

"Well, well," said Roger. "Don't they sell vegetables at these big supermarkets?"

"They sell everything that's eatable," declared Sam. "Talking of supermarkets, Mr. West, I did a bit of checking on Cockell Shops, as you asked me. It's a big board now, with nine directors. Used to be a one-man concern. The original Cockell built it up from one general shop. But he had a bit of family trouble. Son kicked over the traces, married beneath him, and the old man disowned him. That's nine years ago. Two years next November old Cockell died, and his widow brought a lot of new blood into the business. The managing director is a chap named Slessor, but he's only a guinea-pig, really."

"Make me an appointment with Slessor, and Mrs. Cockell," Roger said.

Mrs. Cockell was out of England, he was told, but Slessor seemed glad to see him. He was a tall, rather indeterminate man, obviously worried by the robberies, probably worried by a lot of things. He knew that some dubious characters were employed at the Cockell Shops, in spite of all efforts to prevent it, but no one with a known criminal record was employed. And should one condemn a man, untried?

"But I hope you will give our shops all possible protection, Mr. West. I really do. The matter will be raised at next week's directors' meeting, of course. May I assure the Board that you have the matter well in hand?"

Roger said: "You can warn the Board that if the branches employ dubious characters, these dubious characters might work with raiders, and that you'd be wise to check all your staff."

"Staff is such a problem," Slessor remarked, unhappily.

"Heavy losses through theft could be a bigger one," Roger said, drily. He left, and started on the round of the Divisions. As he drove about London he seemed to see grocery "little man" shops, Cockell Shops and Food Fairs everywhere.

By the time he had been to each of the Divisional Stations, checked all the reports and all the results of the investigations, it was nearly midnight.

He had had some fish and chips at Battersea and was more thirsty than hungry when he started back for Chelsea and home. The cleverness of the organisation and all its implications worried him, and the possible significance of the shells seemed to fade. He did not intend to go back to the Yard, and would probably be home before Janet went to bed, after all; it often happened like that. He listened to the confusion of sounds on the radio, the normal network of requests, news flashes, reports of crimes, reports of arrests, instructions to police cars, all in the background. Then he had a flash:

"Calling Superintendent West . . . Calling Superintendent West . . . Over."

Roger flicked on his microphone.

"Superintendent West is hearing you . . . over."

The man said: "Message for you from Superintendent Baker of Whitechapel, sir . . . A man named Orde, who has been spending some time with Mrs. Endicott, of Brasher's

Row, has gone into her house tonight, been there for the last two hours. Superintendent Baker thought you would like to know."

Roger said: "Yes. Thanks." He flicked off the radio, and drove silently and frowningly for several minutes along the Embankment towards his home. Baker of Whitechapel knew that "Orde" was actually Cyril Owen, of course, and Baker obviously thought it wise that he, Roger, should know what was happening tonight. This probably meant that Baker was worried.

So would Roger be, if Owen spent the night with Ruth Endicott.

Or did Owen think there was no limit to what he should do for the sake of his job?

XV

NIGHT DUTY

"I'LL tell you what, Cy," Ruth Endicott said. "Why don't we buy some fish and chips and take it home, it's ever so much more comfortable there."

"That's a jolly good idea," said Cyril Owen, "but I ought to be in bed early tonight, ducks."

"*I* won't stop you," Ruth promised him.

They were walking away from the Roxy, in Whitechapel Road, just after ten o'clock. The show had finished earlier than usual, and they felt a little cheated. Owen was uneasy because the situation between him and this girl was getting out of hand. It was one thing to scrape an acquaintance—and that certainly hadn't been difficult; he had waited until Ruth came into the Walsh's shop, made the usual joking suggestions about a night at the pictures or at the *palais*, and hadn't really been surprised when after a show of coyness she had said yes.

That had been a week ago, and he had seen her every evening since. He had not yet started to try to find out much about her husband, being sure that he must approach that question cautiously; but a situation had developed which really began to worry him.

In the first place, he was getting fond of Ruth. She had a perky way with her, a nice sense of humour, and a much higher intelligence than he had anticipated. She wasn't clever by any means, and hadn't a great deal of general knowledge, but she certainly wasn't a fool. Many of the girls he had been around with had been morons compared with shrewd little, plump little Ruth.

Her smallness, or rather her shortness, and her plumpness, intrigued him, too. She dressed to fit her figure much more than she had when her husband had been alive, and had a ridiculously small waist—he couldn't quite span it with the fingers of his two hands, but the middle fingers weren't far apart when he tried. She had a swelling bosom, tightly confined, showing a deep cleavage, and her hips curved so that from behind she looked like an old-fashioned egg timer.

More important than any of this was the fact that she had taken to him.

This was their third evening at the pictures, the third of holding hands, the second when she had taken his right hand and guided it to her breast, to her full, soft thighs. Sitting so close to her, with this promise of intimacy, had awakened all the male in him; he had been glad when the film ended and the National Anthem was played.

Now Owen had a real problem.

He was pretty sure what Ruth wanted; sure that she was acutely lonely at night. Her suggestion of buying fish and chips and taking them home meant only one thing—she wanted to get him into the house. She knew that he wasn't married, and knew where he lived and worked, too.

It wasn't often that an attractive girl threw herself at him; usually it took a lot longer than this to make a complete conquest, and Owen did not know what to do. If he made excuses, and didn't go home with her, or if he stayed for an hour and left without any proof of passion and desire, it might be his last chance. He had wanted this affair to develop much more slowly and deliberately, but now he had to make up his mind in a hurry. His attitude could determine the whole of their future relationship, and this was hardly a thing on which he could take advice.

She believed he was shy, of course, and diffident; he could tell that when she took his hands, when she whispered: "I love you touching me," when she looked at him and smiled very knowingly.

He was twenty-seven and she was twenty-four, and there were a lot of times when he felt that she was twice his age.

Half a dozen people ahead of them turned into a brightly lit fried-fish shop, outside which a green fluorescent sign read:

Eat Here or Take Away.

Ruth believed that his hedging was simply due to shyness, remember; if he did anything which made it clear that it wasn't, there was no telling how she would react.

"Come on," she said, as they reached the shop. "The plaice here is ever so nice, and we'll be home in five minutes. It'll still be hot." She held his hand as she pulled him towards the door, and he followed her.

He saw a policeman on the other side of the road, a man who had no idea that he was a plain-clothes officer; he had noticed that the police kept an eye on Ruth. She was smiling, almost laughing, as she went into the brightly lit shop, with its penetrating odour of frying oil and frying fish, the hissing and bubbling as fresh chips were tossed into the boiling oil. The four in front went to the tables, so that he and Ruth were alone at the counter.

If he made an excuse——

"Three plaice and a shillingsworth of chips," Ruth ordered from the dark-haired, dark-eyed Greek who owned the place.

At one end of the counter was a stack of cigarettes and chocolates, just behind the cashier, a grey-haired woman who sat at a small window. The policeman in Owen noticed this, and tucked it away in the back of his mind. The Greek was taking pieces of plaice from the grille at the top of the fryer; a girl shovelled crisp golden chips into a greaseproof bag.

"If I go home with her," Owen told himself, "that's it and all about it." He watched her as she stood at the counter, flushed, rosy-cheeked, excited and happy. He found himself taking out a ten shilling note and paying for the fish and chips. He felt the increasing warmth of the packet as he carried it along towards the next turning, Ruth's arm linked in his free arm. He turned the corner into Brasher's Row, and saw the policeman who had been in Whitechapel Road, walking along with a sergeant; here, even in these days, the police did not patrol in ones except by day.

The fish was hot and beginning to get smelly when they reached Ruth's little house.

"I won't be half a jiff," she said, and let him go, and rum-aged in her bag for her key. He was quite sure that once he was inside he wouldn't be able to resist her; it would be virtually impossible to come away after a meal, anyway.

She pushed the door open.

"Go on in, silly," she said. "I won't eat you!" She gave him a little push, and switched on the light, and they stepped inside. She closed the door, quickly, and looked up at him. She was striking and beautifully coloured, and her eyes were so bright; she was obviously delighted.

She pushed the bolt home at the top of the door, standing on tip-toe to do it, and then took the package from him. "I'll pop this in the oven to keep warm, and lay the table," she said. "How about a little drink, Cy? Would you like a whisky or a gin and something?"

"A—a whisky sounds fine," said Owen.

"I'll tell you what, you help yourself. I'll pop this in the oven and then go upstairs and put some slippers on," Ruth said. "I hate walking about the house in high heels. Wouldn't you?"

"Hate it," he made himself say.

"There's where I keep the drinks," she said, and pointed to a small wall cupboard in a corner. "You needn't be too mean with the whisky, I've another bottle tucked away somewhere." She hurried out of the living-room, the room where she had seen the plump man who had come to her just after her husband's death, and into the kitchen. He heard the pop of gas, saw her bending down at the oven, adjusting the flame, then saw and heard her take down dishes and plates, and heard the rustle of paper. She was an efficient little person.

He opened the corner cupboard and found glasses and the whisky, some gin, a bottle of Noilly Prat and a bottle of Cinzano, as well as some Babychams. He poured himself a stiff whisky, and sipped it. Ruth was out of sight now, and he called:

"What will you have, Ruth?"

"I think I'd like one of those little bottles of Babycham," she called, and a moment later appeared, flushed from the heat of the stove. "Pour it out for me, Cy love." She flashed a bright roguish smile at him as she passed, and touched his hand; then he heard her hurrying up the stairs. He drank more of the whisky, pondering. If he walked out now he would never be able to win her confidence; if he stayed now he might be making serious trouble for himself.

He heard her moving about. He took down two bottles of the "champagne", and hesitated, then took down two champagne glasses.

"I started it, I'll finish it," he said, and tossed the rest of the whisky down. The decision gave him a curious sense of relief, and his heart began to throb. He listened intently, and heard Ruth padding about, presumably in her slippers. She was a long time if she was just changing her shoes. He half finished his second drink, and then heard a soft, rustling sound in the passage; it scared him, and he jumped forward.

She was coming towards him from the foot of the staircase, wearing a flimsy gauze-like housecoat which hid very little, even when she was in the gloom of the passage. As she came into the brighter light of the living-room, he could see through the gauze almost as if through glass. He had never imagined a fuller, firmer, more seductive figure. The delight in her eyes, the promise and the hope, were unmistakable.

"I just had to change, Cy," she whispered, and came towards him. He didn't move. She drew up close to him, and slid her arms round him, pressing her body against his. "Cy," she said, "I can make this couch into a bed, or we can go upstairs. Which would you rather?"

He moistened his lips. "Ruth, that fish'll get baked."

She put her head back and laughed at him, and he saw how white and beautifully even her teeth were. He tightened his grip round her shoulders, and then hoisted her in his arms.

Then he carried her upstairs.

·   ·   ·   ·   ·

"Cy," she said, afterwards, "I hope you don't think I'm terrible." "I think *you're* wonderful."

Owen didn't speak.

"Cy," said Ruth, lying on her side, quite naked, quite lovely, "there's something I've got to tell you."

"Listen, Ruth——"

"I've just got to tell you," she insisted. "I was married to my husband for five years, and I *hated* it. I hated—I hated having to give in to him. I just hated him. I didn't realise anything could be so wonderful, but when I first saw you, I knew—I knew we would just have to get to know each other better. You—you felt like that too, didn't you?"

Owen moistened his lips.

"Of course I did."

"There's something about you," Ruth said, and she half closed her eyes; he had never realised before how curly and long her black eyelashes were. "You—you're the first man I've ever really been interested in, that's the honest truth. After my husband died—after he was murdered, I mean—I didn't think I'd ever have anything to do with men again. I hated them all. I even hated the police—they kept asking me questions all the time, as if they didn't believe me, but they might just as well. My husband's like a bad dream, now, but it wasn't until I met you that I realised I was absolutely free from him, free from everything."

"What about his friends?" Owen made himself ask.

"I didn't know any of his friends," said Ruth, in a low-pitched voice. "I didn't want to, either. Cy, I'm telling you the honest truth, I *hated* him. I just had to put up with him, he frightened me so much. If you knew how he treated me . . ."

It was as if the passion of their union had released some store of memory, as if she had been repressing all these things for a long time, and now had to talk about them. Owen let her talk. She had a soothing voice, and she talked without heat and without venom, telling him how she had hated Endicott, showing him the scars she bore, and he prompted her now and again, so that she went on talking lazily, sometimes taking his hand and fondling it.

. . . . .

It was much later, downstairs, as they ate the fish and chips, which had gone a little soggy, that he noticed the sea shells in a drawer of the corner cupboard, where he was looking for a bottle opener. He didn't give them a thought. There were a dozen of them or more, all little pink sea-shore shells which he noticed as he did everything.

XVI

REPORT

THE morning's reports showed very little advance on those of the night before. Neither of the men caught by Constable O'Hara had yet been identified, and neither had made any kind of statement; they were due at the South-West Police Court some time before three o'clock, but at the moment there was no name under which to charge them. A flimsy paper mask of the kind sold to children had been discovered near one of the raided shops. None of the injured shopkeepers had been detained in hospital. The newspapers used the story as the main lead on the front pages, but there was no editorial comment. He, Roger, was mentioned in every newspaper as the Yard man in charge of the investigation.

He spent ten minutes sticking more location pins into the wall map. At ten o'clock, the door opened after a light tap, and Hardy came in. He was wearing a brown suit, and he looked spruce and a little too well-brushed.

"Good morning, Handsome." Hardy was usually formal, because he had come up from the ranks and his post as Commander sometimes sat heavily on him. "Is there any news? I'm due to see the Assistant Commissioner at half past ten."

"I'll have a brief report ready and typed out by then," said Roger.

"Good. Is there any clue at all?"

"There's a queer little thing which might mean nothing," said Roger, and pointed to the shells. "If Endicott had had one, I'd be more inclined to think they had some significance, but there was plenty of time for anything in his pockets to be removed. I wonder if there are any shells at his house?"

"How about his widow?"

Roger said: "Young Owen's seeing what he can find out from her." He didn't mention the message from Charlie Baker. Hardy studied the winkle shell, the little fan shell and the lobster claw. "There are no prints except those of the two men on anything," Roger went on. "These aren't on our files, and neither will talk. As for the motor-scooters, tens of thousands of them are fitted with luggage containers—that's no help. The sack was home made, of strong plastic."

"Any conclusions?" asked Hardy.

"None at all."

Hardy stood there like a frustrated sergeant major.

"Think it might spread?"

"They worked on four Divisions," Roger said, "and they can have a go at any others they like. The almost certain thing is that next time they'll change the venue. Mass raids on supermarkets could be the next on the list."

"I read your report about the interview with Slessor, of Cockell Shops," said Hardy. "Do these supermarkets have to employ many dubious characters?"

"If each Cockell Shop, or any big supermarket, had one inside man, we could really have big-scale trouble," Roger said, "and they can't be sure whom they're employing. It's too easy to forge a reference."

Hardy shrugged, said: "Well, keep trying," and went out.

Roger sent the sergeant off to make sure the typewritten report was ready, and was alone at his desk when a telephone bell rang.

"West speaking."

"It's Mr. Baker, of Whitechapel, sir."

"Put him through." Roger frowned at the map of Whitechapel but saw a mental picture of young Owen. It was several seconds before Baker came on the line.

"Roger?"

"'Morning, Charlie. What's new?"

"Got a funny thing to report," said the Whitechapel superintendent promptly. "In the first place, Owen spent the night at Mrs. E's place."

Roger said: "Oh, did he!" and the familiar feeling of disquiet seemed to be deeper.

"And he's been on the phone—wants to see you," went on

Baker. "He won't talk to anyone else. He says he's got an extra hour off at lunchtime, so he could meet you anywhere. He suggests a hotel, perhaps the Strand Palace, to make sure that he isn't seen talking to you."

"I wouldn't mind a square meal myself," Roger said. "I'll book a table in the grill room there, in a corner, if you'll tell Owen to meet me at about a quarter to one. Okay?"

"Seems all right," said Baker. "Wish I knew what he was up to."

.   .   .   .   .

Owen entered the grill room a few minutes early, and Roger saw him speaking to the head waiter, who turned and pointed. Owen threaded his way between the tables. He was serious-faced, as if there was plenty on his mind, and looked very young, almost sulky. He was wearing a green tweed suit which made him seem very bulky. When he reached the table he hesitated.

"Sit down," said Roger.

"Thank you, sir."

"We're all right here," Roger said. "I've fixed it so that no one will be near enough to hear what we say if we keep our voices down. What will you have to drink?"

"I'm not particularly anxious to——"

"I'm going to have a lager. Suit you?"

"Thank you, sir."

"And I've ordered some tomato soup, and a mixed grill," Roger went on.

Owen moistened his lips. "That sounds fine, sir, but I didn't intend that you should—er—buy me a meal. I just wanted to talk in confidence, and—well, it's a very deli—very difficult subject, Mr. West."

"I don't mind how difficult or delicate it is, provided I get the truth," Roger said. "Have you made any progress?"

"Yes, sir."

"Go on."

"I don't think Ruth Endicott knows anything more than she told you, except one thing," declared Owen. "Just after her husband's murder and before you went to see her, she had a visit from a stranger, who . . ."

Roger listened to the story which Ruth had told Owen last night.

Owen looked almost dazed, although he spoke vividly and simply as he went on: "In my opinion, there isn't any doubt that she was too frightened to tell you about this, sir, and I don't think there's any doubt that she's alive because she convinced this man that she didn't know anything about Endicott's business. I believe she's absolutely in the clear, sir."

"Then you've done a good job," Roger said.

"Have I?" asked Owen. He looked down at his empty soup plate, and was about to speak when the waiter glided to the table with the grill on a silver plated dish, while another man whipped away the soup plates. The helping of steak, kidney, liver, bacon, sausage, and lamb cutlet was huge; the pile of chips, here called French fried, reminded Owen vividly of the fish and chips last night.

"It sounds a good job," Roger declared. "We know the kind of man to look for, and if we ever find him, Mrs. Endicott can be used to identify him."

"I suppose so," Owen said, and waited until the waiter had gone. Then he looked Roger squarely in the eye. "The truth is, sir, I feel all kinds of a swine. You see, last night I—well, I spent the night with Mrs. E. I won't beat about the bush, but I'm telling you this in absolute confidence, sir—you needn't report it to anyone else, need you?"

"No. I'll keep it to myself."

"Thank you, sir. Well, I won't beat about the bush. Ruth— Mrs. E.—fell for me soon after we met, and it was she who stepped up the pace. If it had been just an ordinary *affaire* I wouldn't have had any complaints, but—well, I suppose the truth is that she's been damned lonely—affection starved, in a kind of way. She—she had a rough time with her husband, and—well, anyhow, whatever the cause, she set the pace. I had to go along with her, or risk upsetting her so much that I couldn't hope to find out what I was after. It was fifty-fifty in a way, though—I'm not going to try to tell you that I exactly—er—hated it. But this morning I feel all kinds of a swine. Sooner or later she'll have to learn that I'm a copper."

Roger said slowly, heavily: "I can see your problem." He started to eat, and was intrigued when Owen sliced a sausage in half, and put a half into his mouth. There was cause for satisfaction that Owen had volunteered this story; on the other hand, there was the official problem as well as Owen's. He could imagine how this story could be exaggerated if it ever reached the Press; for instance, how it could be made to look as if Owen had deliberately seduced Ruth Endicott in the course of his duty.

He could imagine what Hardy would say. He could see photographs like those in the weekly magazine, the voluptuous widow and the unscrupulous police. It was useless to think that the story could never leak out. It need not; but if this Endicott woman was spiteful—which was possible, if she had fooled Owen, as she probably had—she might have plenty to say when she discovered that he was a detective.

"You'd better come off the job right away," Roger said. "At the first opportunity, when the danger for Mrs. Endicott is over, try to make some kind of explanation." As he spoke, Roger felt that it was an unsatisfying response to a kind of S.O.S. call, and obviously it did not greatly help Owen.

"I know that's one way to handle it," said Owen, "but I'm not sure it's safe."

"Safe?"

"For Ruth," Owen said.

Roger looked at him steadily, wondering what was really in his mind. Owen gave him time to think by eating a piece of now cold liver, and went on:

"We know what kind of people we're up against, Mr. West, don't we? And they're thorough, too. We can be darned sure that they're still watching Ruth—in fact I think I know who they're using. If I suddenly disappear from the shop and from the district, they're likely to assume that I was just there for a job; I think they'd take it for granted it was a police job. I'd hate to think what they would do to Ruth, if they once thought that. They'd certainly work on her to find out what she'd told me."

Roger said, in a taut voice: "Yes, you're quite right." He hadn't seen it that way, and for a few moments he was shaken; but slowly the one really satisfactory aspect forced itself forward. Owen was proving very good. He could look at a problem and turn it inside out; despite the emotional factors, he missed nothing.

"So what the hell *am* I to do?" Owen demanded.

Roger pushed his plate away. "Give me time to think about it," he said, and waved the waiter away. Owen was still eating. "What's this about the man who is watching her?"

"He's another newcomer to the district," declared Owen. "He's just bought a shop near Brasher's Row. It used to be owned by an old couple, who got past it. He bought it a couple of weeks ago, did it up a bit, and now he's canvassing for trade. He's making special price offers, and going all out to build up the business—and he's particularly interested in Ruth E."

"Sure?"

"He calls on her for orders every day, and doesn't do that with anyone else," said Owen. "She's quite amused by it in one way, a bit nervous in another. She doesn't like him, particularly. Every time she goes into the shop—it's where she gets most of her oddments, being very handy—he's all over her. Asked her to have a drink with him two or three times already. Damned funny thing," went on Owen, in that semi-cultured voice of his, "that she should fall for me, and react against him. I've seen the chap. He's a bit older than I am, I'd say, got a beard, quite good-looking in a way. Of course she feels that he's watching her for this other man, and it's scared her. As a matter of fact, Mr. West, I did wonder whether it would be a good idea if we persuaded Ruth E. to get out of the district until it's over. I mean, if I were to tell her the truth—or if you were to, and advise her to take a holiday, I think she'd jump at it, she's so scared."

Roger thought: "If *I* talk to her!" but he showed no reaction, and considered the idea on its face value; it proved again that Owen could use his mind, and it was probably as easy a way out of the immediate difficulty as they could find. In fact it was almost too easy.

"If this chap's bought the shop fairly recently, it wasn't to watch Mrs. E.," he pointed out. "She could be watched without that. But if he's particularly interested—here!" His voice rose. "What's this chap like? What kind of build? How old do you say?" He rapped the questions out in quick succession. At first Owen was startled, but he answered each one to the point.

"He's around thirty-five, I'd say. Five feet ten or eleven. Fairly broad-shouldered, grey eyes, fairish hair. Has a beard, and it curls slightly. Ruth says that he's not new to his job. He knows groceries all right—my God!" It was Owen's turn to break off, and stare. "Are you wondering if this is the missing grocer, Stone?"

"Yes."

"Well I'm damned!" exclaimed Owen. "Wouldn't have given it a thought, but now you've pointed it out, he could be Stone. I'd soon see, if I saw Stone's photograph with a beard pencilled on."

. . . . .

In the middle of that afternoon, a man called at the Walsh's shop ostensibly to get a bicycle puncture mended, and showed Owen *alias* Orde a photograph of Stone, plus a beard. Owen simply said: "That's the shopkeeper who calls himself Simpson, no doubt about it."

The word was passed to Roger within an hour. He was so intrigued by it that he forgot the one thing he had failed to ask Owen. In a way, it was a key question: had there been any sea shells at Mrs. Endicott's house? There was some excuse for the failure, for he had never been busier, and he was at the special late court at half past four that afternoon, for the first hearing against the two men whose names were not yet known.

Both refused to plead, and both refused to speak; they were remanded for the usual eight days, and taken to Brixton Prison for the period of the remand. The late evening and morning newspapers carried big photographs of them, under the heading:

DO YOU KNOW THESE MEN
If so, communicate at once with
the nearest police station or
telephone Whitehall 1212.

. . . . .

"While I'm waiting for results to come from this, I've got to decide what to do about Owen and his Mrs. E.," Roger said to Janet, when he got home that evening. She was the one person whom he could safely tell about Owen's story, and also the one most likely to offer some useful advice.

"There isn't any question, you've got to send this Ruth E. out of London," Janet declared briskly. She listened, because she thought she heard one of the boys approaching from the front room, where they were at their homework; was satisfied that neither was coming, and went on: "Don't sit there saying nothing, Roger."

"Can't think of anything to say for once."

"What you mean is, ought you to let her stay in Brasher's Row, and see what happens between her and Stone or Simpson or whatever he calls himself now?" said Janet. "My pet, even for the sake of finding out who's behind all this, you can't take risks with that young woman. That's no way to be a policeman. You've got to get her out of London."

Roger was still pondering when a man from the Yard called to say that the cashier of a Cockell Shop in the Battersea Bridge Road had telephoned to identify the two raiders.

"Both were employed there," the Yard caller said. "Looks as if this gang could have men planted everywhere, doesn't it? Before we know where we are, there could be mass raids with thousands of quids being pinched every time, instead of a couple of hundred."

XVII

SECOND VISIT

RUTH ENDICOTT was happier on the morning after her night with Cyril Orde than she had been for many, many years. She felt that they were right for each other, and had felt so almost from the first time they had met.

There was something about the smile in Cy's brown eyes, the way his lips curved when he was looking at her, the unexpected things he was always saying, which attracted her. It did not occur to her to wonder why he had suddenly come to work at Walsh's; in fact it did not occur to her to ask questions about him at all. She took him as he was.

While she was making the bed, she was humming to herself. His pillow was pushed up against the head panel, the indentation of his head very plain. Suddenly, exultantly, she snatched the pillow up and hugged it and kissed it—and then she tossed it away, laughing, and said aloud:

"What would he think of you, you little goop!"

She finished making the bed, ran the vacuum cleaner over the wall-to-wall carpet, and stood at the doorway looking at the wall mirror on her side of the bed. This morning, she had kept on a wrap while she had got out of bed, a queer little quirk of shyness which now amused her.

It did not occur to her that she might have done anything wrong; she was free, she owed nothing to Endicott's memory, she had no friends, no children, no relatives who mattered, and she felt a sense of rightness and of permanence about the friendship with Cy.

She went down the stairs in flat-heeled shoes and into the kitchen, where an hour before she had fried him bacon and eggs. She switched on the radio, made some fresh coffee, looked through the newspapers, then became absorbed in a magazine. The time slipped by. It was past twelve o'clock before she got up, stretched and yawned, scolded herself for laziness, and attacked the washing-up with a sporadic vigour which characterised much that she did.

She felt that she could laugh at the whole world.

She was putting the rinsed dishes in the drying rack when there was a knock at the front door. She hesitated before turning round. Who was that? Not the insurance man, he had called two days ago. Not the milkman, he'd been. Everything else she went out to buy.

"Oh, no!" she exclaimed. "It's that man Simpson."

She went quickly along the narrow passage, but instead of opening the front door went into the tiny front room, and approached the window. Simpson's three-wheeler van was parked outside. She didn't want to see him, especially this morning, but suddenly decided that it wasn't his fault that she didn't like him; she hurried to the door. He was waiting, smiling expectantly. She felt a twinge of conscience, he looked so pleased to see her.

"Good morning, Mrs. Endicott! I was passing, and I thought I would see if there was anything you wanted?"

"Well, no, not really," Ruth said. "If there's anything I've run out of, I'll pop into the shop."

"It's no trouble to deliver anything you want," Simpson assured her. She sensed there was a kind of anxiety in him, as if he could not take no for an answer; and in a way that reminded her of how Endicott had been before she had promised to marry him. Simpson put his left foot forward, and whether by intent or not, stopped her from closing the door. "As a matter of fact, Mrs. Endicott, I've got some special offers, and if you'd care to look at the list——"

She couldn't very well be *rude* to the man.

She let him come in, and he ran down some lists of canned groceries and preserves which he carried with him; but she saw that he was looking round the living-room with even more interest than Cy had done. He was about the same age as Cy, and much better looking, while the beard made him quite distinctive; why was it she didn't like him? He brushed her bare arm with the back of his hand, and glanced at her sharply; she felt a little uneasy about his being here.

"Don't make up your mind now, just think about it," he said at last. "If you care to order the big supplies in one go, it will save you at least two shillings in the pound. And you've got plenty of storage room, haven't you?"

He looked round again, as if making sure that he did not miss anything.

"Thank you ever so much," said Ruth. "I'll tell you in a few days."

"Any time, there's no hurry," said Simpson, and then he asked: "Don't you find it lonely, living on your own?"

"No, I quite like it, really."

"You don't look the kind of person who enjoys living by herself, you look much too friendly," Simpson declared. He had given up all pretence of trying to sell her goods, and was looking at her intently from across the living-room table, leaning against the back of the chair on which Cy had sat for his breakfast. "But then, I suppose you've a lot of friends."

"No, not really," she said idly, and then wished she had said that she had hundreds. "Well, of course, I've got plenty—I'm not at all lonely."

"I suppose your husband had a lot of friends, and you see them from time to time."

That was the moment when Ruth first began to wonder what he was really getting at. Questions about Endicott always worried her; the only time she had been able to talk freely about her husband had been last night, with Cy. This was different. This man had no right to force his way into her house and start asking questions like that.

"I suppose that man who works at the cycle shop was a friend of your husband?" said Simpson.

Ruth drew in a deep breath. Her anger must have shown in her eyes, for Simpson backed away a pace.

"No, he wasn't. And what right have you to come in here and ask me a lot of questions? You're being downright rude, that's the truth of it. Get out of my house." Ruth pointed towards the door with that touch of the dramatic which came naturally to her, and was too angry to see how startled and shaken he looked. When he simply stood gaping, she raised her voice: "Get out of my house at once, and don't come bothering me again!"

"No, please," he said, chokily. "No, Mrs. Endicott, I—I didn't mean to bother you. I didn't mean——"

"Don't just stand there. Get out of my house!"

"I'm terribly sorry, terribly," Simpson said. He spoke so brokenly that he almost made Ruth feel sorry for him; but she was still quivering with indignation, and did not relax. He started along the narrow passage, opened the door, and then muttered: "I really am sorry. I wouldn't upset you for the world. I do hope that you won't—won't take your custom away. I promise you that I won't make a nuisance of myself again."

"We'll see about that," she said, standing squarely in the hall.

He turned and went back to his van, miserably. She closed the door with a snap, and then hurried into the front room, to see what he did. He reached the door of the van, and stood for a moment with such a look of dejection that this time she really felt sorry for him. Then he got into the van, and drove off.

. . . . .

Ruth felt a little guilty and uneasy when Simpson had gone; after all, he had gone to a lot of trouble, and she had seldom seen anyone look more dejected. It worried her rather until, late in the afternoon, she found a note from Cy lying on the doormat, and then all she could think about was Cy. Wasn't he going to see her this evening? Had he regretted anything?

He had written:

"There's a very urgent rush job in the shop for tonight, ducks. Could you find me a snack supper if I come round for half an hour about eight o'clock?"

She could not have been more delighted had he sworn undying love.

He was his usual gay self during the half hour they spent together, made some sly, intimate references to last night, and said that he didn't intend to work late too often, even for the Walsh's. She walked back to the shop with him; the light in the workshop was on, and Walsh was also working. She returned to her house, turned on the television, and watched every programme on the commercial channel. Then, yawning and happy, she went to bed.

Next morning, there was a letter in the post—from Simpson, the grocer. He had a small, very upright hand, and his words were stiff and formal:

"Dear Mrs. Endicott,

I am extremely sorry if I caused you annoyance or embarrassment. I wish to assure you of my very deep respect and admiration.

I wish to assure you also that all my questions are purely on your behalf. I have recently suffered a great personal loss, and am only too well aware of how lonely a person can feel.

I am going to trespass on your good nature, and will call upon you again today, with certain supplies of goods at special prices.

Yours respectfully,
J. Simpson.

In a way it made her want to laugh; in another, to cry. But she couldn't refuse to see the man after a letter like that.

When he arrived, he was most polite and anxious not to cause offence, and Ruth was equally polite. She had just made some coffee, and out of natural good nature, offered him a cup. He accepted eagerly, and she went into the kitchen.

It was by sheer chance that she came away before the coffee was made, and saw him bending over her husband's desk, with a drawer open. She was so angry that she actually ran at him, striking at his arm—and she had never seen a man more taken aback. He stammered apologies, and allowed her to bustle him along the passage and outside. He seemed to stagger before he reached his van, but recovered, got in, and drove off.

Then she saw another man sitting in a car across the road,

hidden until then by the van. It was the fattish man who had come to see her just after her husband's murder.

.   .   .   .   .   .

All thought of Simpson vanished from Ruth's mind. She stood rigid with the kind of fear which she had almost forgotten. The man watched the van as it moved along the street, and then turned his head and looked across at this house.

Ruth began to breathe heavily. She saw his expression, that nasty smile, the smile which had terrified her. She thought: "*Cy!*" and her mind began to work on one thought only: the thought of escape from this man. She didn't want to see him again, she didn't want to talk to him. *Why was he here?* She felt almost hypnotised as she stood by the window, dreading the moment when he would come across the road towards her, but he didn't move. She moistened her lips, and turned away from the window; at first it needed a great physical effort. She reached the passage and ran up the stairs and into her bedroom, kicked off her house shoes and put on others, slapped a small hat on the side of her head and pushed a red-headed pin through it, and put on a light summer coat. All she could think about was seeing Cy, telling him that she was frightened of this man.

She looked out of the window; he was walking along the street.

She thought: "It's all right, he's going," and yet her mood of panic did not go, that single glimpse of him had frightened her so much. She grabbed her handbag, and hurried down the stairs, turned towards the kitchen and picked up a shopping basket.

Why had this man come back? Why had Simpson come and asked questions about her dead husband? She remembered all the questions which the man across the road had asked her, how he had warned her not to talk about his call, or about her husband's activities—and he had been nervous in case she talked to the police.

Was Simpson a policeman?

She opened the front door, and stepped out, glancing right and left, half afraid that she would see the man near the house and on this side of the street. He was nowhere in sight.

She slammed the door behind her, feeling rather silly with relief. It *might* have been coincidence. At heart she believed that it had not been, though; there must be some reason for the man's return—and the reason seemed to be connected with the new grocer. She had never liked that man with the beard. If he was going to get her into trouble, she would hate him.

She turned right, away from the shop, but the quickest way to the Whitechapel Road, and Walsh's place. It was a quarter to one. She would pop in to see Cy about her bicycle, any excuse would do, and if he were alone in the shop she would tell him what had happened and ask his help; she felt so sure that she could rely on that.

She saw Mrs. Walsh, a short, dumpy, dark-haired woman, enormous with child, at the counter. Her heart dropped.

"Well, no, Mrs. Endicott," said Mrs. Walsh, "Mr. Orde's asked for an extra hour off today, and he went to lunch early— he's got some relatives up from the country, he says. But he'll be back by half past two, he promised me. Can you come back, if it's something only he knows about? My husband's in the workshop, but . . ."

"It isn't important, really," Ruth said. "Any time will do."

She left the shop, feeling rather foolish, went along the main street, bought some sausages and a piece of frying steak from a butcher who did not close for the lunch-hour, and some apples and Jaffa oranges from a barrow boy. Then she started back for home. Her panic had subsided, and she was half inclined to laugh at herself.

She opened the front door with her key, stepped inside, closed the door—and then screamed.

The fat man who so frightened her had stepped out of the front room, within arm's reach.

XVIII

LITTLE JOURNEY

"I shouldn't make a noise like that again, or you'll really get hurt," said the plumpish man. "Come here, Ruthie."

She didn't move.

"Ruthie, I told you to come here," the man said, and moved towards her. In panic, she swung round and snatched at the handle of the door, but before she could turn it, the man was at her back. She felt his hands slide round her neck, felt the strength of his fingers on her windpipe and the pressure of his thumbs at the back of her neck—awful, agonising, even worse because she couldn't breathe. He was forcing her back against him at the same time, and she could feel hot breath on her hair.

She tried to struggle and kick, but could hardly move.

She tried desperately to draw breath, but could not; all that happened was a tightening band round her breast, great pressure there, at her eyes, at her forehead and at her ears, which seemed to get tighter and tighter. She believed he was going to kill her. She felt a kind of darkness descending and thought it was the darkness of death.

Then he eased the pressure.

She reeled away from him, and leaned against the wall, taking in great gulps of air, hardly able to realise what had happened. Her neck hurt. Her lungs hurt. She could not see, because there was such a mist in front of her eyes.

The man said something, but she did not know what it was. She felt a touch on her shoulder and tried to shrink away, but the man shifted his grip, took her arm and forced her to turn round, then made her walk in front of him into the living-room. The searing breaths which racked her body echoed, quivering, about the walls. He let her go, and she supported herself against the table, then edged round towards her chair and collapsed into it. Her breathing became easier, but her fear no less.

Gradually, the round head and smooth shoulders took on shape and clarity. Ruth's breathing was almost back to normal. The man held something out towards her, and she saw that it was a drink. She took it, her fingers trembling, sipped, then drank it down; it was a strong whisky and soda. It brought tears to her eyes, and the effort of swallowing hurt. She leaned back in the chair, seeing the man sitting on a corner of the table and watching her from narrowed eyes.

"Ruthie," he said, "you've got to tell me all about your love life."

She didn't answer.

"And if you tell me the truth you'll be all right," the man said. "If you lie to me, you'll get hurt, Ruthie. You'll get hurt, and then you'll go on a little journey, the kind of little journey that your poor hubby went on. Do you get me?"

She managed to nod her head.

"Now who's the all-conquering boy friend, Ruthie? Who's the lug you slept with last night?"

"He—he doesn't know anything!" she gasped. "He's just a friend, that's all, he's just a friend." She hardly knew what she was saying, she was so desperate to make sure that this man did not do anything to hurt Cyril. "He—he works at a cycle shop in Whitechapel Road, at Walsh's. He—he's just a friend."

"So that's how you entertain your friends," the man answered. "Butcher, baker, cycle-maker, and we mustn't forget the grocer, must we? What about that bearded boy friend, Ruthie?" The man leaned forward and put out his right hand, and although she tried to get out of his reach, she could not. He caught her chin between his thumb and forefinger, and pushed her head back, so that she had to look into his eyes. "I didn't think you had it in you. One lover-boy here all night, and another here by twelve o'clock next morning. Poor old Lionel would turn over in his grave."

"It's not—it's not true," she gasped; the pressure at her chin made it difficult to get the words out. "He—he—he just came to sell me some groceries."

"Don't lie to me, Ruthie," warned the man in front of her.

"He's called here most days, and you've been in the shop a couple of times. Isn't that true?"

"Yes, yes, but——"

"And he's not come to bring you a pound of sugar or a quarter of tea," sneered the plump man. "What's he been here for, if it wasn't to lay you?"

She was gasping for breath, but did not try to answer.

"Listen, Ruthie," went on the plump man, "are you setting up house for any man with money in his pocket? Are you turning this into a whore-shop?"

"*No!!*" she managed to scream, and wriggled herself free and jumped up. "*Get out of my house!*" She struck at him as he tried to grab her again, and by chance pushed him heavily to one side. He slipped off the table, and couldn't save himself. He was between her and the door, and she had to get out; she was terrified, she had to have help. She could think of nothing but getting to the door, but if she tried to jump over him he would stop her. She saw him, wedged between the table legs and the wall, scrambling to get up; he was in an awkward position, which gave her a few precious moments of grace. She ran round the other side of the table as the man got to his feet, and he was still out of reach. She pulled open the door—and ran into another man standing there.

He was grinning.

She recoiled, too shocked for words. He blocked the doorway: a man whom she had never seen before, short, squat, swarthy. Her hands were raised to fend him off, and for that split second thought of the plump man was driven from her mind.

She felt hands brush the back of her head again, and remembered the way in which she had nearly been strangled. She tried to twist round, but the man behind her did not try to strangle her this time. Instead, he buried his fingers in her hair, and began to pull, slowly, powerfully, until the hair was straining away from the scalp; a different kind of pain and a different kind of fear took possession of her. She felt him pulling savagely. She knew that he was forcing her head back, too—so that her throat was arched. She saw the man in the passage grinning; and she saw him put his right hand to his waistband. It wasn't until he drew his hand out that she realised what he held.

The blade of a knife stabbed out.

"*No!*" Ruth screeched.

"Ready for her, Fats?" the man with the knife asked. He ran his thumb along the blade, as if testing the sharpness, and he grinned so that she could see all his teeth. "How about doing it in one, eh?"

"Oh, God, no, don't kill me, don't kill me!"

"Never have done it in one yet," the man with the knife said. "I'm ready to try." He raised the knife, holding it sideways, as if he were going to slash.

"Put that away," said the fat man behind her. "She's coming on a little journey with us." He let her go, but held her by the shoulders, or she would have collapsed, sobbing. "Hear that, Ruthie? You're coming with us, and when we get you to a nice quiet place you're going to tell us all about your lover boys, and what they've wanted to know, and what you've told them."

She only just heard what he said.

"For instance," said the plump man, "have you told them about the shells?"

She thought vaguely: "Shells?" She didn't know what he meant, hardly remembered that her husband had often carried sea shells in his pocket, as if he collected them.

"You got them from the cupboard?" asked the man with the knife. He hadn't put his weapon away yet, and his expression seemed to say that he was reluctant to.

"I've got 'em," the plump man said. "The car outside?"

"Yeh."

"Go get the engine started," ordered the plump man, and as the man pressed the knife handle and the venomous looking blade snapped back into it, Fats took a hold on Ruth's arm, just above the elbow, and gripped her very tightly. It hurt, but its worst effect was to warn her how much pain he could cause if he intended to. "Ruthie," he said, "you've got to tell us everything. Every damned thing. If you don't——"

He broke off.

After a pause, the sound of an engine starting up came clearly.

"Now you just walk with me to the car and get inside, and you don't make any fuss," the plump man said. "If you make any fuss, you won't ever see the light of day again."

·   ·   ·   ·   ·

As she stepped across the narrow pavement to the car, Ruth looked desperately right and left, but no one was in sight. It was about two o'clock, a quiet hour. If she could have seen Cy, just caught a glimpse of him, nothing would have kept her from crying out; but the street was empty, almost picturesque in the warm summer sunlight and against the clear blue sky

She got into the car.

The plump man climbed in beside her, held her wrist, and said:

"Okay, George."

The car slid along Brasher's Row, and turned two corners, including the one where Simpson's van stood outside. Ruth thought she saw the man's fair head through the shop window, but he didn't look up, and if he had she probably would not have tried to attract his attention.

The plump man was saying: "Just do as you're told and you won't get hurt." After a pause, she felt him fumbling in his pocket, and then she saw him take out a pair of dark-lensed glasses. "Put these on," he said. "Then you won't be able to see where you're going, will you?"

She put them on unsteadily, and darkness descended on her. She could just make out the outlines of the street, the people, the shops and the houses. Once they were on the main road, the car put on speed.

She did not know how long they were driving, but it must have been over half an hour, often through thick traffic. Then she realised that they were driving through a different kind of district; there were big houses, a few fields, fewer people. She heard the dear, sweet singing of birds, and the leisurely clatter of a lawn mower. Then the car swayed to one side, and she was thrust against the plump man, who gave her a squeeze, and laughed as if he felt on top of the world.

"Now we're there," he said. "You can take off your glasses."

The house was double-fronted, with beautiful bow windows on either side, and rose beds out into fresh close-cut lawns: roses of pink and yellow and white, of red and mauve and scarlet.

The man who stood in the doorway was middle-aged. He had a most distinguished appearance; although the bright sunlight hurt Ruth's eyes after the period of darkness, she could not fail to notice that.

Fats, still holding her arm, said: "We got her."

"So you got her," said the distinguished-looking man. He stood in the doorway, without smiling, staring at her as if at an exhibit. "I see," he said at last. "Put her in the morning room. I want a word with you."

"Okay," said the plump man.

The house had high ceilings. The big staircase was panelled. There were big oil portraits on the walls. The floor was of dark wood, with some skin rugs on it, including a tiger skin almost real enough to be frightening.

Ruth was just aware of these things as the plump man named Fats led her to a door which stood ajar. He pushed open the door and thrust her into a small, sunlit room, with big windows overlooking a beautiful green lawn and a wide border of flowers. It was so beautiful, so restful and so peaceful, that the sight of it momentarily eased her terror.

Ruth heard the clear chiming of a clock, a pure note which seemed to come from nearby. It struck three. There was no clock in here. While she was looking round, she heard the man speak in a quiet, clear voice, although some distance away. She could hear what was being said in the next room.

Her heart began to beat faster. She stared towards the sound and saw another door open an inch; the men in the other room probably didn't know that. She went closer. The beauty of the garden, the sight of the flitting birds, the quiet voices and the fact that she could hear what was being said, all worked together to give her hope.

A man was saying coldly: "We should have found this out before. Shell won't like it. Simpson isn't Simpson at all. He's Stone, the husband of the woman Endicott killed. A newspaperman recognised him, there's a story in the *Globe* today."

Ruth caught her breath.

"I told you there was something fishy about him, didn't I?" asked Fats, but it did not dawn on Ruth that he was on the defensive, nervous of the other man. "I thought maybe he was a cop."

"You should have found out," said the man. "Have you any more information about the man in the cycle shop, what's his name?"

Ruth wanted to scream: "*No!*"

"No," said Fats, almost sullenly. Fearfully?

"Then it's time you found out," said the distinguished-looking man, coldly. "Do you think he's a detective?"

Ruth thought: "*No, no, he can't be!*"

"He doesn't look the type," answered Fats, "but he might be."

"He took the job only two weeks ago, and these Walsh people know nothing about him, do they?"

"They said they didn't."

"So he arrived out of nowhere," said the man. "Don't waste any more time finding out whether he's a policeman or not. Quite obviously he is. How do you think Shell will like this?"

Ruth was leaning against the arm of a big chair; she felt as if she was going to faint.

Fats said: "I did all I could, I tell you. I used Endicott to get rid of the Stone woman, and put Endicott and Gantry away because they could have named Shell. What more does she want?"

The man said smoothly:

"She told you to get rid of Endicott's widow."

"But it was throwing money away!"

"It was disobeying orders," the man said, "but it might be

an advantage to have her alive. Do you think this Endicott woman knows who Orde is?"

"I'll soon find out," said Fats. There was a vicious note in his voice, a note which Ruth recognised only too well. With her, he was the big shot, and all-powerful; with the man here he was only a servant, and both men seemed dominated by this unknown Shell. "If Orde's a cop, and Ruthie knows it, she'll talk all right."

"It shouldn't be difficult to make her," said the other. "Use the old air raid shelter. If she kicks up a row she can't be heard from there."

"Want me to start work now?"

"Why don't you tell her what you want, and give her an hour to think it over?" the man suggested. "It's always better to get information without using strong-arm methods. But I don't care what you have to do to make her talk, so long as you find out everything she knows about this Orde, if she's been working with the police, and if she's told Simpson-or-Stone anything. Get the lot, if you're to justify yourself with Shell."

"I'll get it, don't you worry," Fats promised. It was as if he was turning the screw on to a wound already agonising, causing pain where greater pain seemed impossible. So much was being thrown at Ruth; the suspicion of Cy, the truth about Simpson, the fact that these men suspected that she was working with the police, the fact that Fats was obviously prepared to torture her to make her tell the truth.

Would he believe her when she did tell it?

She heard footsteps.

"And Fats——" said the distinguished-looking man.

"Yes?"

"What are you going to do with her afterwards?"

"I'll take care of that," Fats said. "I'll forget her dough."

"You will have to be extremely careful."

Fats gave a short, high-pitched laugh.

"I've already dug a deep hole," he said.

The other man made no comment. There were more foot-steps, and then a door opened and closed. The footsteps faded.

Ruth leaned against the arm of the chair, staring at the partly open door, knowing that the passage door would open at any moment, knowing that there was nothing she could do to save herself from the man named Fats.

But——

The distinguished-looking man who could talk so cold-bloodedly about hiding her body, did not know that this second door was open.

XIX

AMENDS

ALTHOUGH no one had harassed her about it, Detective Sergeant Bella Dawson of the C.I.D. felt very badly indeed about her failure to keep track of Jim Stone. It had seemed such an easy assignment, and she was acutely aware that her own carelessness had been partly responsible for what had happened. Consequently, she spent much of her off-duty hours trying to find out where Stone was. Obviously Brasher's Row and Mrs. Endicott's little house were possibilities, and she spent some time near Brasher's Row, explaining her presence to local shop-keepers and the landlords of two public-houses as she had explained it to Stone.

She was a journalist, looking for sob stories.

Although she caught sight of the man Simpson several times, at the wheel of his van or inside his shop, it was not for some days that she learned he had only just bought the business. That made her very curious, and she was anxious to get a good look at the man, but three days after she had first visited Brasher's Row she was sent to an urgent job in Wimbledon. There two young girls had been assaulted, and women police were particularly required. She did not tell Chief Inspector Ethel Winstanley about her suspicions of Simpson; she meant to be absolutely sure of her ground before she told anyone. A second mistake would be hard to live down.

The first chance she had of going back was the second morning after Owen *alias* Orde had spent the night with Ruth Endicott. Bella Dawson knew nothing of that, of course, and her main interest was in the grocer from the corner shop. She did not want him to see and recognise her, so she sat behind the windshield of a motor-scooter, wearing a pale blue crash helmet and a pair of dark-lensed goggles, as well as a pair of tight jeans. Girl scooterists like her were two a penny all over London. She watched when the grocer took his

van out, followed him, and saw when he pulled up outside
Number 37.

She watched him get down from the van, and that was the
moment when she felt jubilant. Something about the way
he moved gave him away; she was quite sure that it was Stone.

What was he doing with Endicott's widow?

Bella Dawson waited until the man had gone inside, and then
drove round the block so that she could see the house from the
other side and a different corner; she was less likely to be
noticed that way. The van was still there when she stopped
again. She pushed her crash helmet back and dabbed her forehead, for it was very warm, and she wondered how shiny her
snub nose was. In fact, she looked oddly attractive as she sat
astride the machine, studying a book as if planning a list of
houses on which to call.

She saw a car turn into the road. A plumpish man got out,
and strolled along on the side opposite Ruth Endicott's. At
first she took little notice of this individual; it was no longer
remarkable that people who lived in this kind of slum district
owned cars. A man was left at the wheel of the car, and she
began to wonder what they were doing. Then she noticed that
the plump man kept looking towards the grocer's van; he
walked up and down with the van as the centre of his pere-
grinations.

By now, Bella was very alert indeed.

She wrote quickly in the loose-leaf book she was using, tore
the page out, folded it, and tucked it into the top of her belt.
Simpson-Stone was still in the little house, and she began to
wonder why; was Endicott's widow going on the loose? Bella
wasn't very interested about the other woman's morals, but
felt sure that she was on to something; the presence of the
plump man and the car made her feel even more sure. She
started the engine of the scooter, and drove along Brasher's
Row and past the van, past the plump man, who took no
notice of her, and the driver of the blue Austin. The driver
whistled as she went by, and she tossed her head. She turned
the corner, slowed down, waited until a lorry came from the
docks so that she could switch off her engine without the

silence being noticeable, and parked at the side of the road, just round by the shop. Book in hand, she went to the corner.

As she reached it, Simpson-Stone came out of Mrs. Endicott's house.

One thing was certain at the first glance; the man wasn't very happy. Bella was some distance away, but had seldom seen a man look more dejected. She heard the door slam, and Simpson-Stone paused for a few seconds by the side of his van, looking more dejected than ever. As if with a physical effort, he climbed back into his van, and started off. As soon as he had gone, the plump man raised a hand, obviously in signal to the driver of the car.

Was Simpson to be followed?

The driver started his engine, and drove slowly towards 37, Brasher's Row. For a few moments, Bella Dawson thought that the men were going inside, but the plump man went to the car and got in, and the car moved off.

This was bewildering; they hadn't followed the grocer and weren't going into the little house. Why were they so interested? A tinge of disappointment took the edge off the detective sergeant's excitement, but she could use a little time. She started the engine, scooted along to the Whitechapel Road, and saw a policeman standing on a corner looking with resigned interest at a massive traffic block. Huge diesel lorries, engines still clanking, waspish little cars, enormous buses growling and crawling. The air was blue with fumes which hazed the rooftops, the stench was sickening and the hot sun made it all intolerable.

Bella wheeled the machine close to the policeman, and without getting off she said:

"Take this note and telephone it to Scotland Yard, will you? To Mr. West or Miss Winstanley. Better do it through the Information Room."

She handed the surprised constable the written message and drove off, approaching Brasher's Row from yet another direction. As she drew near it, she saw the Austin car drawn up close to the corner; beyond it, a woman was walking. She recognised Mrs. Endicott, who disappeared into the Whitechapel Road just beyond a builder's yard where stores of sand, gravel, cement and timber were kept. As she vanished, the two men got out of the Austin car and walked into Brasher's Row.

Three minutes later, Bella Dawson saw them go into number 37; she wasn't sure, but believed that they used a key. She went back and took up a position just inside the builder's yard.

She could see number 37, and be sure when anyone came out. Her excitement and anxiety had reached its height, and as she had sent a message to the Yard, the obvious thing was to wait and see what happened next.

The plump man who had driven the car before came out of Mrs. Endicott's place, walked to the car, and drove it back into Brasher's Row. Bella had an impression that everything he did was carefully calculated; like the shop robberies. Now and again she left her hiding place and looked up and down the several streets, half expecting to see plain-clothes men, but no one came, and she felt no sense of urgency. It would probably be wiser for the Yard to have these men followed, not tackled when they were here. The builder's yard was a godsend.

She bobbed down behind the brieze block fence when she saw Ruth Endicott coming along, waited until the woman had turned the corner into Brasher's Row, went to the corner and watched her go indoors.

She was going to have a shock.

Bella said uneasily: "I don't know whether I ought to leave her or not. She might be in bad trouble."

The policewoman was out of her depth, partly because of her awareness of the first failure. Quite suddenly she decided that she must not leave the Endicott woman alone any longer. The men involved in this case were ruthless killers. If they murdered Ruth Endicott, it would be on her, Bella Dawson's, conscience for a long time. She made up her mind what to do; tell the first man or woman who came along to telephone the police for urgent help, and then go to Number 37.

She stepped out of the entrance of the builder's yard, and saw a man coming from the Whitechapel Road; she didn't greatly like the look of him, but he would have to do. She didn't need to give him a message; all he had to do was make sure that the Division sent men round to 37 Brasher's Row.

"Will you please——?" she began.

It was something in the man's eyes which warned her of impending trouble, and on that instant she was ready for it— but she wasn't ready for the man who came vaulting over the builder's yard wall behind her. She snatched at her whistle, tucked inside the waistband of her tight pants, but before she could get it out, the man behind hooked her legs from under her and the man in front struck her on the side of the head with a piece of iron bar. The side of the helmet saved her, but she felt herself picked up, one man carrying her arms, the other her ankles, sensed that she was being taken deep into the yard. She tried to cry out for help, but her throat seemed to close on itself. She felt herself being swung to and fro, as if she were the third person in an acrobatic trio. One man holding her ankles, the other her wrists, they swung her higher and higher.

Her breath seemed to be trapped in her throat. She was gasping, fighting, choking for breath. There was nothing she could do to stop this or to save herself. She had the awful fear that at any moment they would let her go, and send her crashing on to the ground or against the wall.

She heard a man say: "On three."

"Okay."

No, no, no!

"*One*," the first man said, and now she felt herself being swung even higher, and it seemed as if the men were making the final effort to hurl her as far as they could.

"*Two*."

The pressure was agonising at her throat, her head was whirling, her ears throbbing. She just heard:

"*Three!*"

Then they let her go. She felt the relaxation of the pressure at her wrists and ankles, felt herself sailing through the air, dreaded the thought of crashing into brick or cement, so that her whole body would be crushed. Then she thudded against something which hurt, and yet did not crush or break her. She didn't know what it was until something small and gritty got into her mouth, and she realised that they had flung her against a heap of sand. She lay spread-eagled, head stabbing with pain, ears throbbing, heart pounding, body twitching spasmodically.

Then she felt a single heavy blow on the back of her neck, and lost consciousness.

.   .   .   .   .

She did not know what followed; did not know that the two men were shovelling the sand, and burying her in it.

.   .   .   .

The police constable who had taken the message from the motor-cyclist wasn't altogether surprised, for he knew there was a lot of plain-clothes activity in the neighbourhood. But he soon had other problems. Two private cars and a lorry, all driven by impatient drivers, got into a tangle. Two front wings and some headlamps were smashed, and the accident put the traffic into a greater tangle than ever. The constable spent fifteen minutes helping to sort it out, but took the first opportunity to go to his nearest police box and telephone the Division.

"All right, Cartwright," said the sergeant he talked to. "I'll pass it on. It's for Superintendent West or that woman Winstanley, you say?"

"That's what the girl on the scooter said, sir."

"Right. Now, what's the message?"

The police constable read the message slowly and with great deliberation:

Message from D. S. Dawson, C.I.D. S.Yrd. Reason to believe grocer Simpson corner Brasher's Row and Liberty Street is James Stone of Clapham. Also reason to believe two men very interested in Endicott widow. Do not recognise either men but one is the type involved in shop raids. Earlier today I saw both men in Cockell's Stores, Whitechapel Road, in assistants' white jackets. They were last seen in dark blue 1959 Austin Cambridge saloon registration number 21JB35.

.   .   .   .   .

Roger West was not in his office when the message arrived, and his sergeant had been sent out on an urgent job. Chief Inspector Winstanley was having a late lunch. The Inspector in charge of the Information Room pondered on the best thing to do; he knew West too well to do nothing, but was anxious not to take precipitate action.

"I know what I'll do," he decided, and wrote out an instruction, then handed it to one of the teletype operators. It read:

Watch for and report position of dark blue Austin Cambridge 1959 model. Registration number 21JB35.

XX

S.O.S.

ROGER came into his office a little after three o'clock, eased his collar and loosened his tie, and looked across at the sergeant's deserted desk. Holidays meant a lot of dislocation at the Yard and the concentration on the Shop Robberies job had not helped. He sat at his own desk, dabbed his forehead with a handkerchief which looked grubby, and thought fleetingly that if Janet knew he had come without a clean one, she would read him the riot act. "Reading the riot act" reminded him of the woman sergeant, Dawson, and he grinned. Ethel Winstanley had told him that her Bella was spending most of her off-duty time in the Brasher's Row area, and if she discovered the truth about Stone *alias* Simpson she would probably regard it as a triumph.

Then he saw her message; the third one on the pile. He read it once, and then more thoroughly. Before he had finished, he lifted a telephone and asked for *Information*.

"Who took the message from Bella Dawson?" he demanded.

"It came through Charlie Baker's uniformed boys," *Information* told him.

"Any news of that Austin?"

"Eight or nine reports in, so far. It's been going East, last seen on the borders of Epping Forest."

"Who's in it?"

Information said: "Half a mo'."

Roger waited, skimming through some of the other messages. There had been no more reports of shop burglaries, and nothing else to help trace the stolen goods. The total cash loot was higher than he had anticipated, nearly nine thousand pounds. The cigarette losses came to a little under four thousand; it was big business as well as big crime. He began to feel impatient, when *Information* came on again.

"Four reports say there were two men and a girl, the other

reports don't mention the occupants, just the car. There's a report just coming over the teletype, skipper. Like to hold on?"

"Yes," said Roger. He thought: "Two men and a girl." There was an obvious possibility that the girl was Ruth Endicott, but that was wild guessing.

He saw the time of the first message from Bella Dawson—twelve-forty-five. Why hadn't she reported again? That was over two hours ago. He lifted up another telephone, said: "Get me Mr. Baker of Whitechapel," and sat with a receiver at each ear.

"You there?" Excitement quickened the *Information* man's voice when he spoke again.

"What is it?"

"That car's been traced to a house called Forest Ley, the home of the late Llewellyn Cockell," *Information* said. "Cockell's widow owns it, and a man named Slessor lives there."

Roger said: "Good God!"

"My sentiments exactly! An Epping copper saw it turning into the drive, no doubt about it. According to this he telephoned his station within five minutes of seeing it, and the car's still there."

"Right," said Roger. "It might mean a lot or it might be a false scent, but we'll assume that it means business. Have Forest Ley covered—better have the whole approach area cordoned off, and station a few plain-clothes men within easy reach of the house. But don't take any other action yet, and don't let anything happen to make Slessor think we're interested."

"Right."

"I'll want a report before I leave here, too, say in ten minutes, and reports all the way to Epping."

"Don't tell me you're going there?"

"Just concentrate on those reports," Roger ordered. He rang off and hoped that Charlie Baker would not come on too soon; he needed time to think. Cockell's stores were all over London and Southern England, all on supermarket lines, like

the one in the Whitechapel Road. Mrs. Stone managed the
hostel where many of the London staff lived.

Mrs. Stone——

Charlie Baker's Cockney voice sounded in his ear, and
Roger wrenched his thoughts off Mrs. Stone.

"Charlie, has Bella Dawson reported again?"

Baker didn't answer.

"You there, Charlie?" Roger demanded sharply. He was
in no mood to be patient.

Baker said: "Yes, I'm here. Had a hell of a kick in the pants,
Handsome. No, she hasn't reported. Won't ever report
again, either."

Roger felt his heart begin to beat very fast.

"Now what's happened?"

"Her body was found only ten minutes ago, buried in sand
at a builder's yard. A lorry driver went to pick up a load of
sand, and found her. She'd been knocked on the head. Our
divisional surgeon's with her now."

Roger didn't speak; he knew exactly how Baker had felt
when he had first come on the line.

Baker said painfully: "Done anything about that dark blue
Austin?"

"Yes, we've traced it," Roger answered. "To Slessor, the
chain-store man. Send round to Ruth Endicott's place, and
check there—break in if you have to—on the ground that we
believe the woman might have been injured. Better pick up
the man Stone, and see what he can tell us. Have Mrs. Stone
watched, at her hostel. I'll be at Brasher's Row in about half
an hour—on my way out to Epping."

"Right," Baker said.

Roger rang off, paused for a moment, lifted the telephone
again, and put in a call to the cycle shop at Whitechapel Road.
It was a long time coming through. He called the Commander
on the other line, and reported briefly; as he rang off, a woman
came on the first telephone.

"It's Walsh's Cycles, here."

"I'm sorry to worry you," Roger said, "but I need to speak
to Mr. Orde, urgently. Is he there, please?"

"Well, yes, he's in the workshop," the woman said.
"But——"

"I wonder if you'll give him a message," said Roger, for time began to worry him. "Ask him if he'll meet me, my name is West, at 37 Brasher's Row in about twenty minutes time."

"But—but he's working on a rush repair. He——"

"I'm Superintendent West of New Scotland Yard, Mrs. Walsh, and need to talk to Orde urgently."

"All right, sir," the woman capitulated. "I'll tell him."

"Thanks very much," Roger said. He stood up, fastened his collar, snatched his hat off a stand, and went out. He put his head round the door of the nearest sergeants' room, and said: "Will someone let Information and the Commander know that I'm going to Brasher's Row, and then out to Epping? We're interested in a house called Forest Ley."

A chorus of "Yes, sirs," came after him.

He hurried down into the yard, took his car, and swung out on to the Embankment, his box beside him, his mood as black as it could be. Despite the news about Slessor, of Cockell's, he could not concentrate on that angle, but kept seeing mind pictures of Bella Dawson, with her clear skin and snub nose, and the twinkle that had seemed to lurk in her eyes. The girl couldn't have been more than twenty-five or six, and she was smart or she wouldn't have reached sergeant's rank.

Roger flicked on his telephone.

"Send a message to Dr. Appleby for me," he told *Information*. "If he can examine the body at the builder's yard at Whitechapel Road, I'll be grateful."

"Right, sir."

"Thanks," Roger grunted. He rang off, and concentrated on driving. It was one of those afternoons when traffic was fairly clear, and when traffic lights seemed to work especially for him. He went via Tower Hill, not the Bank, and once in Aldgate, he saw two of Cockell's stores, with the clear lettering, the big display windows, the wire baskets, the cashiers at their little counters.

Then he thought, almost absurdly: "Cockleshells all in a row." The line from the old nursery rhyme seemed to strike with painful force. Cockell—Cockle shells. Shells, shells, shells!

He was approaching the junction of Whitechapel Road and Mile End Road when his radio picked up:

"Calling Superintendent West—calling Superintendent West. Over."

"West here," Roger said. "West answering. Over."

"Information calling, sir. The cordon has been put round Forest Ley, and the Austin car is still in the drive of the house. Mrs. Cockell is said to be out of the country. Mrs. Stone is not in her office or in her apartment. No one has gone in or come out of Forest Ley since our last report, and all approaches to it are now closed. Are we to hold anyone coming out?"

Roger said: "Yes."

"Are we to raid the house itself, sir?"

Roger said: "I'll call you. There's another urgent surveillance job. If necessary ask Commander Hardy to arrange to transfer men from the other London Divisions. We want every one of Cockell's stores watched."

Information made a choking sound.

"And the Cockell hostel, not just Mrs. Stone," Roger said. "Don't raid any places, just watch, especially for men who answer the descriptions of the shop raiders."

"Right."

"If Mr. Hardy has any misgivings, ask him to call me at Whitechapel," Roger went on. "Anything else for me?"

"Dr. Appleby is on his way to Whitechapel, Mr. West."

"Thanks," Roger said. He rang off, and turned the next corner.

Just ahead was an ambulance, several police cars, a cordon of police across the road, and a crowd of at least fifty people. Policemen cleared a path for him and he went into the builder's yard. The girl was lying on her side, in a strangely relaxed attitude, as if she were asleep. In the tight-fitting blue jeans and the green linen blouse, she looked very small and very young. Someone had wiped her nose, eyes and mouth, but the sand still clung to her hair, ears and neck. A police surgeon was examining her wrists. Divisional men were bending over footprints in the yard, and others were examining the gate posts. The lorry driver who had found the body was standing by his tip-up lorry in a corner, still looking pale. Charlie Baker came massively across to Roger, pushing his hat to the back of his head, his round face burned almost to a mahogany colour, his fringe of curly hair making him even more like a painting of a saint without his beard.

Roger said: "How about the Endicott widow?"

"Gone off," said Baker.

"Anyone see her go?"

"A neighbour saw her leave with two men, who drove off in a car. That blue Austin Cambridge, for certain," said Baker. "I've talked to Stone. He says he tried to find out some information about her husband, and she flared up and gave him marching orders. He's still at his shop. Want to see him?"

Roger was looking over the heads of the crowd towards two men who came hurrying; one of them was young Owen, *alias* Orde, bare-headed, eyes glinting, chin thrust forward.

"Not yet," Roger said. "If Mrs. Endicott didn't work with these people, she's been kidnapped." It was strange to find the word come out so dispassionately. "In any case, we want her in a hurry."

"If she's alive," said Baker.

Roger looked down at the slight, still body of Detective Sergeant Dawson, as Owen came pushing his way into the yard. A Divisional man said: "Don't tread on that footprint!" Another muttered: "Mind your big feet." Anxiety made Owen look almost distinguished as he drew up, but he waited for Roger to speak.

"Mrs. Endicott's been taken away," Roger said. "We know where she is."

"Then what are we standing here for?" demanded Owen, harshly. "Where is she?"

Roger said: "She's at a house in Epping, and the Epping police know where."

"Why isn't the house being raided?" Owen forgot that he was talking to a senior officer.

Roger said: "It will be raided when we're ready." He looked at Owen very straight, realising that the man was desperately anxious to go to the rescue of the woman. That kind of reaction was natural, but there was a better way for Owen to help. Roger had a sense of inevitability, that Owen had been fated to take a part in this as well as to become emotionally involved.

Roger went on: "Take it easy, Owen, I've a job for you soon." He could tell from the man's tense expression that Owen expected to be put on to a stop-gap job, but he didn't retort, and Appleby came up, wearing an old alpaca jacket and a straw boater. He looked at the group gathered about the dead policewoman, went down on one knee, and inspected the hands and the ankles.

The police surgeon from the Division said:

"I can't make those marks out, Dr. Appleby. Can you? See the snag marks round the ankles of the stockings? All the ladders start there. And then the marks round the wrists——" he broke off.

Appleby went squatting down. A car engine started up. People at the back of the crowd were talking noisily, and a policeman said: "Move along, there, make a gangway."

"Yes," said Appleby. "They're f-f-finger-marks, not rope or card marks. See the mark of the f-f-finger-nails just here?" He pulled the leg of the jeans up a little, and showed three crescent shaped marks on the fair clear skin. On the stockings were some greasy looking marks, and he put his nose down and sniffed. "B-b-bacon fat," he announced. "The man had just handled fat bacon." He stood up, went to the side of the sand, and pointed to some marks. "Looks as if this b-b-bit's been left undisturbed. See the mark? Two men swung her to and fro, holding wrists and ankles, and then l-l-let her go. She landed there. With luck, she was almost unconscious by the time she landed."

"I've checked the place where she was struck on the back of the neck," the Divisional Police Surgeon put in quickly. "She was unconscious when she was buried."

"Yes," said Appleby. "Unconscious but b-b-b-buried

alive." He straightened up. "Handsome," he said, "we've
always known this was an ugly job. We can see it's even ug-ug-
uglier. How many men were involved in the mass raids?"

"Sixty-six, at least."

"They wouldn't use every man they'd g-got. There must
be eighty or more."

"Yes," Roger said.

"Know the leader yet?"

"We think we know a bit," Roger said cautiously. He
pushed his hair back from his forehead, thinking how near
Cockell's store was, that the killers had probably come from
there. But he mustn't be precipitate; he had a big job to do.
"The leader's got Ruth Endicott a prisoner." He broke off,
looking into Appleby's eyes, fully aware that Baker was
puzzled by his manner, that Appleby was too, while Owen
looked both mutinous and sullen. "The main job is to
pick up all those eighty men," he said. "If we don't, then we'll
be coming up against them for years. See my problem?"

Appleby nodded.

"But if Slessor of Cockell's is the man, and you pick him
up——" Baker began, but stopped as if understanding dawned
on him.

"The usual method would be to cut off the head and let the
limbs wither away, but can we?" Roger demanded. "Dare we?
Think how many killers there are involved. Look at what's
happened here." The grease spots on that sheath-like stocking
seemed to show up more vividly as he looked down. "If they
lose their leader they'll lie low for a bit, but they'll start again,
because——"

He didn't finish.

"Trained to it," Appleby said.

"What is this?" demanded Baker, and one of the Divisional
men muttered something under his breath. Traffic rumbled in
the distance, and a policeman said again: "Move along there,
move along."

"What this is," declared Appleby, looking even more boyish
than usual, "is the established fact that sixty or more trained
crooks are at large. They might be warned, and split up

into ones and twos. That's Handsome's worry. Is there a way of c-c-catching all of 'em in one go? Eh, Handsome? If there is, it will justify t-t-taking risks with the Endicott girl. That it?"

Roger said: "That's it."

XXI

POKER

INTO a tense silence, Baker said: "You mean they're specially trained to kill."

"Some of them, I'd say," said Appleby. "That's been Handsome's worry from the beginning."

"But surely——"

"Nothing remarkable about training men to kill," said Appleby. "We're doing it all the time. How old are most of the ch-ch-chaps we've had reports on?"

"Early twenties," said Baker.

"Don't doubt they got their training in the armed f-f-forces," said Appleby. "Some leader of men selected those without consciences, the natural killers, and g-g-got 'em together." He glanced down at the pale-blue stillness of the dead policewoman. "If the photographers have finished, there's no reason why she shouldn't be moved."

Roger sensed that he was making a diversion to allow more time to think, and Roger certainly needed it.

Appleby was absolutely right; he had a nose for a situation like this, and could see it in proper perspective. Baker couldn't. Young Owen might be able to, but didn't want to, this time, because Endicott's widow meant a lot to him. But the basic and frightening fact remained: there was an organised army of thieves trained by men without scruple or conscience.

"Mr. West, if you can't make up your mind——" Owen began.

Roger said: "Take it easy. George," he went on to Baker, "let's go to 37 Brasher's Row. We can talk more freely there."

"Talk!" cried Owen. "Who the hell wants——"

Roger said coldly: "Don't get under my feet, Owen." He moved towards the gateway, the police cleared a path among the gaping crowd, and in less than five minutes they took over

the house in Brasher's Row, filling it to overflowing, and with
hundreds of sightseers already in the street.

Roger, Baker, Appleby and Owen were in the living-room
with the doors closed. It was unbearably stuffy, and Owen had
a wild look.

"Now that we can talk without being overheard, let's get a
move on," Roger said briskly. "Owen, if we raid this place in
Epping, anyone there might be warned. If they behaved in
character, they'd first kill Mrs Endicott and fight their way out.
There's just one way we might be able to get most of this mob
in one place."

Baker said: "I can't see it."

Appleby was smiling faintly and holding his ancient straw in
one hand, and picking at the ribbon with the other.

"Owen," said Roger, "whether we like it or not, you're the
key man in this. We know from the Walsh's that these people
have been asking about you. They know the situation between
you and Mrs. Endicott. They guess you're a policeman.
That all puts you in a special position. See that?"

Tightlipped, angry from the rebuke, Owen said: "Yes, sir."

Appleby was nodding and smiling and picking.

"What we've got to do is to draw these killers into one spot."

"Think they'll just walk into the parlour?" Baker asked, but
now Owen looked at Roger very intently, all anger gone.

"Owen, I want you to telephone Slessor," Roger went on.
"I want you to tell him that you know where he lives, and you
know that Ruth Endicott is there. I want you to tell him
exactly who you are, and to say you're not reporting to the
Yard yet—that you'll keep quiet if he'll let the woman go free."

"He'll never buy it!" cried Baker.

"Look what he'll think he's b-b-buying," interposed
Appleby. "A day's grace at least, and a chance of security.
Go on, Superintendent."

Owen's eyes now held a curiously bright glitter.

"If Slessor does the obvious thing, he'll ask you to go to this
house on your own," continued Roger. "First to prove you
really know where he is, second to try to make some kind of
deal. He'd cut your throat and the girl's as soon as he was

clear, but if you can make him think you'll go alone, he may let you in. Once in, you'd have a chance to look after Mrs. Endicott, and to trap the mob. You'd be gambling with your life, mind you."

As he spoke, Roger thought bitterly: "I wish to God I could gamble with mine." In fact, Slessor might believe that a man of Owen's rank was corruptible, but he would feel almost sure that Roger wasn't.

"I'll gamble," Owen said, after a moment's pause. "But how will this get his killers all in one place?"

"If you tell Slessor that at shop closing time tonight, we're going to have each Cockell shop raided, and are going to pick up all the assistants who can't prove where they were between four and six o'clock on the day of the mass raids, he's almost certain to warn any guilty men to get away before the raid. He's likely to have a rendezvous where he gives them orders, and where the loot is delivered. It's almost certainly in central London. We'll watch Cockell Shops from the time you telephone, find out where the men are going, and wait until we can pick them all up together."

Roger broke off. Baker pushed his hat further to the back of his head, and Appleby said: "Quite a b-b-brainwave, Handsome."

"But Slessor will kill Owen and this Endicott girl the moment he knows that Owen's fooling him," declared Baker.

"That's the risk," Roger agreed. "That's why Owen is going to be ready for trouble. Knowing what is likely to happen will give him an odds-on chance." He was watching Owen closely as he went on: "Ready to take this chance?"

"Take me to Epping as fast as you can," said Owen huskily. "Just get me to a place where I've got half a chance to get Ruth out of trouble."

.   .   .   .   .   .

After Owen was on his way, Roger talked to Hardy by telephone. The Commander took his time before saying: "I think you're justified in all you've done, and in taking the risk. I'll check with the Assistant Commissioner at once, and get back to you in time for you to stop Detective Constable Owen if the Assistant Commissioner disagrees. How long can you wait?"

"Half an hour at most," said Roger.

"Very well," said Hardy.

It was a long half-hour, but no warning came through.

.   .   .   .   .

About the time that Roger was talking to the Commander Ruth Endicott moved across the small room, where she had listened to Fats and the other man. She was feeling dreadful, for Fats had bellowed and threatened her wildly. Very cautiously, she pushed open the door of the big room, and looked inside. This room was much bigger than she had ever seen in a private house. It seemed to be a mass of books, shelves, glass and dark furniture. As in the hall, the floor was of wood, with skin rugs on it. In one corner, sideways to her, was a large flat-topped desk, with a huge globe by the side of it; sitting at the desk was the grey-haired, distinguished-looking man whom she had seen before.

Almost at once, the passage door opened, and a woman came in. She was well-dressed and well made-up, with a quality which Ruth recognised and could never hope to equal.

The man said:

"Hallo, Shell. I'm very glad you've got here."

"It's time I came," the woman said. "This could be very dangerous indeed. Has the Endicott woman talked?"

"No, but——"

"Does she know what the shells are for?"

"According to Fats, she didn't know a thing about them, or anything that Endicott did. She——"

"Andrew, I think it's time I took over," the woman said. "She was married to a man who got too clever and greedy. He did all right, he got a thousand for fixing Mabel Stone, and then he decided to find out who I was, and why a small sea-shell was used as a code." She was almost sneering. "We agreed that Endicott knew far too much. Remember?"

"Shell, I know——"

"You forget that I thought of that. I planned it all, and

simply left it for you to carry out," the woman went on. "Now you ask me to believe that Endicott didn't even tell his wife how he made so much."

"Shell, Fats said——"

"I told Fats to kill the woman, but he left her alive hoping to get his hands on her money—the money her husband had blackmailed out of you and me. If he had killed the woman, as I told him——"

"Shell, we have to face the situation as it is, not as we would like it to be."

"And I'll face it my way," Shell said. "You'd better go and pack, in case of emergency. Send Fats to me."

The man hesitated, then went out. The woman went to the desk and sat down. Ruth pushed the door open a little wider, and ventured through, her thoughts racing with the wild hope of getting across to the passage door without being noticed. Her heart was thumping so painfully that she felt sure the woman must hear it, but she kept on writing.

In the huge fireplace, with seats on either side of it, were big, brass fire irons. Ruth was nearer them than the desk. She tip-toed towards them, looked round, then bent down and picked up the poker. It was very heavy, and she nearly dropped it. She recovered, but it quivered in her hands. The woman did not look up, but there were sounds in the next room, and suddenly Fats' voice came through the door behind Ruth.

"*What the hell!*"

Shell glanced up, startled—and saw Ruth. For a split second, she was too astonished to speak. Ruth stood with the poker in her hands, half-way between the fireplace and the door. There were hurried footsteps in the morning room, and the door was thrust open.

"She's gone——" the fat man exclaimed, and then he saw Ruth.

"Don't come near me," Ruth said shrilly. "Don't come near me. I'll bash your brains out if you do."

She backed towards the passage door. Both the others were in front of her; the only danger was that the fat man would run across the morning room and into the passage that way. She took another step backward. She saw that Shell's right hand was out of sight, and felt a sudden fear; that she was getting a gun.

"Don't—don't get up, don't move!"

She took another step nearer the door. The others seemed transfixed, and she couldn't really understand it. She was within three or four steps of the door, now, and tried to remember how far away this room was from the front door. It couldn't be far. She was gasping as if she had run a long way. It couldn't be far, it——

The door opened. Slessor appeared in the doorway, and stood watching her. She raised the poker and jumped towards him, swinging the head of the poker down, but Slessor dodged, and the metal banged and boomed against the door. She heard Fats say: "*The bitch!*" She flung herself at Slessor, but he simply put out his right hand and fended her off, pushing her so violently that she went reeling back into Fats' arms.

Fats grabbed her wrist and began to twist.

"That's enough, Fats," said Shell from the desk. "Just take her out and try to reason with her. She might be more useful than you think."

Fats eased his grip on Ruth's wrist.

"Don't kill me," she begged. "I—I heard what you said you were going to do, don't kill me."

"What happens to you will depend on what you tell us," said Shell briskly. She stood up from the desk, looking distinguished and even benevolent, certainly not brutal or vicious like the men. "Give her a cup of tea and let her think things over for half an hour."

"But I don't know anything! I don't know——" Ruth began in terror.

"Come on, Ruthie," urged Fats, and he tightened his grip on her arm again. This time the other woman did and said nothing to stop him. Ruth was half led, half pushed out of the room and into the hall, along the hall and through a doorway at the far end, which led to a narrow passage, and, she saw, to part of the garden. Old raincoats and hats, umbrellas and walking sticks were near this door, and a row of wooden pegs, half of them empty. Slessor opened this door, and Fats urged Ruth forward. This was a side of the garden. She could see the smooth green lawn, a bed of flowers—and the earthwork which was built around an old air raid shelter. The entrance to the shelter was dark and narrow.

"No!" she gasped. "No, I——"

Fats moved closer, thrust his left arm round her mouth and choked the words, and then pushed her towards the air raid shelter entrance. She stumbled at the top step and would have fallen had he not saved her. He flicked on a light, and the darkness of the staircase was brightened by a yellow glow. The steps looked as if they were often used. There was a turn in them.

"Please don't make me——" she began.

"Stop yapping," said Fats, and pushed her down to the turn in the stairs, then down another short flight; there was a door at the foot, standing wide open. Light beckoned, beyond. He gave her another push, and she staggered through the doorway. Instead of coming after her, he grabbed the handle, and pulled the door to. She heard it close with a heavy thud, and she was alone in a small room, no more than six feet square, with plain bare walls, a wooden bench, a chair, some oddments she didn't recognise. She stood staring at the door for what seemed a long time; then the light went out.

She was in pitch darkness.

"No!" she screamed. "No, let me out, let me out!"

She flung herself at the door and began to beat upon it with her clenched fists, but there was only a solid, thumping sound. The door did not yield at all, and there was not a crack of light.

"Let me out, let me out!" she cried.

There was only the echo, mocking her.

.   .   .   .   .

The woman called Shell looked up from her desk, half an hour later, when Fats came in. She studied the man closely, without speaking. Fats stood quite still, and at attention. Slessor wasn't there. It seemed a long time before Shell said:

"You see what a fool you were not to kill her when you had the chance."

"Well, I thought——" Fats began.

"You thought you could make a few thousand on the side," Shell said, but there was no venom in her voice. "Now listen to me, Fats. Endicott was far too dangerous, and Gantry made a hash of the Marsh raid. They both had to die. I got Endicott to do a little private work for me, before he died. The only risk after that was Ruth Endicott. She's been alive long enough to have talked to the grocer or the policeman. Go and find out exactly what she's said to them. I don't care how you do it—just find out."

"Right away," Fats said. "She'll tell us all right, but"—he moistened his lips—"we had a bit more trouble."

"What kind of trouble?"

"We were watched and followed from Brasher's Row," said Fats, and saw the alarm and anger spring to the woman's eyes. He went on hastily: "But we were covered all right. There was a woman on a motor-scooter, a woman cop. One of our boys at the Whitechapel shop saw her snooping around the place some time ago, and she——"

"What happened to her?" Shell interrupted.

"The—the boys put her away. She couldn't have had time to send a message to anyone, but—it means we've killed a woman cop. You ought to know."

"Yes," said Shell, very softly. "I certainly ought to know." She gave the impression that she would like to strike the man. There was another long silence before she went on: "How do you know this woman police officer was alone?"

"The boys said——" began Fats.

Then the telephone bell rang on the big, leather-topped desk. Fats started. Shell looked at it, then stretched out her hand, as if to make sure that nothing was going to shake her out of her habitual calm. She lifted the receiver and said:

"This is Mrs. Llewellyn Cockell."

"So it's Mrs. Cockell," a man said harshly. "Where's Slessor?"

"He isn't here."

"He'd better be."

"Don't be absurd," Shell said quietly. "He isn't here, but I can speak for him. Who are you?"

The man said roughly: "My name's Orde, otherwise known as Owen. Detective Constable Owen of New Scotland Yard." There was a fractional pause before the speaker's voice rose higher; Shell clenched the telephone so tightly that her knuckles went white. "Is Ruth Endicott all right?"

Shell waved her left hand towards another telephone, and Fats reached across and picked it up. As he did so, slowly and deliberately, so as not to make a noise, the caller went on:

"I tell you if you've hurt that girl——"

"Mr. Owen," interrupted Shell, "I really don't know what you are talking about."

"Find out from Slessor," Owen said. "One word from me and you and your mob will be rounded up, you won't have a chance to escape. But if Ruth——"

"I don't think we have anything to discuss," said Shell, "but if you really think this woman Ruth is at my home, why don't you come and see for yourself?"

Owen said: "Don't make any mistake. I can get you and all your men. If it wasn't for Ruth Endicott——"

He left the sentence in mid-air.

"Why don't you come and see me?" suggested the woman, smoothly. "Shall we say in half an hour? Where are you?"

"I'm at Loughton Post Office," Owen said. "I'll be at your place in ten minutes. And listen. I'll be back here with Ruth within the hour, or nothing will save you."

He rang off.

XXII

DEAL

FATS put down his telephone slowly. Shell put hers down heavily, and stared at the man. For the first time emotion showed in the woman's face; there was pallor at her lips. Her make-up showed more vividly; so did the wrinkles at her eyes. She began to breathe shallowly, and when she spoke her lips hardly moved.

"What do you know about Owen?"

"He—he took the job at Walsh's," Fats said.

"What else?"

"He—he looked a funny guy, dressed up in—in plus-fours, tartan socks, brogue shoes——"

"I'm not asking about his sartorial habits. Did you watch him closely?"

"Yes, of course."

"How often did he see Ruth Endicott?"

"Nearly—nearly every day. That's what first made me wonder about him. He was a pushover for her."

"Do you think he is in love with her?"

Fats said: "He—well, he spent a night there."

"A man has been known to spend a night with a woman without being in love with her. Has he any money?"

"He didn't seem to have much."

"Do you know anything about him as a policeman?"

Fats' tongue appeared for a split second, then disappeared. "No."

"How did he behave with Ruth Endicott?"

"He—he drooled over her," said Fats. "I tell you he was a pushover."

"He wasn't the only man interested in a widow with a pile of money tucked away," said Shell. There was now some colour in her cheeks; the look in her eyes was less baleful. "She is the type who could make a man do anything to sleep with her."

Shell rubbed her hands together softly, making a faint sound; she did not look away from Fats. "We haven't any time to find out more about him. How many policemen can you buy?"

Fats said: "Here and there you can buy one."

"Is Owen the kind to sell himself?"

Fats didn't speak.

"You heard what Owen said. What would you do?"

"I—I would—I suppose I would——" Fats broke off.

"Don't tell me you're out of ideas."

"I'd look around, check if there are any police cars nearby, and find out if—if there's a cordon round the house."

"How long will that take you?"

"Shouldn't take long."

"Send Rawson," ordered Shell, and motioned to the door.

Fats hurried across to the hall, and went out, calling: "Rawson!" in a high-pitched voice.

Shell stood up, and went to the window overlooking the lovely garden: the roses still in profusion, a bed of dahlias unbelievably beautiful in colour. Some small bushes, long since bright with flower, grew in a slanting bank which covered one side of the air raid shelter, hiding it from here. She rested one hand on her hip, stared at the bushes and the close-cut grass bank. She was standing like that when Fats came in.

"He's checking," he said, huskily.

"When this man Owen gets here, bring him straight in," said Shell. "I'll talk to him myself. You keep quiet. If he is followed, let me know by raising your right forefinger to your chin. Like this."

Fats nodded.

"If Rawson finds out that we're being watched, raise your left finger to your chin in the same way."

"I know," Fats said. "I know."

"Have you hurt the Endicott girl?"

"I haven't marked her."

"If I want her here, I'll tell you," said Shell.

"Sure, Shell."

"And, Fats," went on Shell, very softly, "I paid you a lot of money to make sure that a thing like this couldn't happen. It wouldn't have happened if you'd killed the Endicott woman when I told you to. Don't argue with me any more."

"You're the Boss," Fats said.

"Remember it. Now go and make sure that we can send messages round to the shops if we need to. We may have to send an alert."

"I'll have the operator standing by."

"See to it," Shell said.

Fats went out, and Shell turned round from the window and went to the desk. She sat down, picked up a pencil, and began to draw faces in profile. A clock on the mantelpiece was ticking away, clearly, loudly, and outside there was the hum of a car engine. She didn't look about.

In a room at the back of this house was a small control room for telephoning all the Cockell branches, and a teletype which had a direct line to them all. Shell knew that Fats would make sure that all routine business was cleared, that all the shops were told to stand by to receive a message. In every case, the Assistant Manager would take it.

She heard a motor-cycle engine roaring, and now her head jerked up. It sounded much louder, and seemed to have turned into the drive. She pressed her pencil against the paper, so that the point snapped. The engine of the motor-cycle stopped, and the silence seemed intense. For a few seconds nothing happened; then she heard footsteps in the hall, so the front door bell had rung. She pushed her chair back and stood up again.

Voices sounded in the hall.

"Mrs. Cockell will see you," Fats said.

"You bet she'll see me," said another man in a clear, half-cultured voice; not quite a full Cockney, but not affected. The door opened, Fats appeared for a moment and said: "Here's the man Owen," and Owen strode into the room. He was wearing gingery plus-fours and bright tartan socks. His hair was dishevelled. There were dried tears on his cheeks and in the corners of his eyes, from the fast motor-cycle ride. He came striding towards the desk.

"Where's Ruth Endicott?"

"Mr. Owen——" Shell began.

"Don't let's waste any words or any time," Owen ordered. "I know she's here. I followed the Austin. My job was to follow her wherever she went. Your blind idiots didn't know that. Where is she?"

"She seems important to you," Shell said, speaking very smoothly.

"She's important enough," Owen said. "She's a darned sight more important to you."

"Really, Mr. Owen——"

"Really, Madame Cockell," said Owen, putting hands on the desk, and leaning closer to the woman behind it. "I'm a cop. Understand that? I'm a cop. I'm working on the Shop Robberies. I know everything that's happened, and I'm on the inside. If you don't hand Ruth over, you won't see another night out of prison."

Fats stirred, just behind Owen, but did not speak.

"And supposing this Ruth were here, supposing——?"

"Don't try to fool me," said Owen. "I saw her come in. I followed that car. The driver might not have seen me, but I followed it. I have to report to West of the Yard at five o'clock. It has to be by five, that's zero hour. If I don't, he'll move in at five to find me. If I report, he might hold off for an hour, to give me a chance of breaking in by myself."

Shell said, slowly, tensely: "I don't know what you mean by moving in or holding off."

"Don't you?" jeered Owen. "That's what I'm here to tell you. West knows all about the Cockell shops, and where your bloody murderers work, and where the cigarettes and where the money goes—in Cockell's shops. It's the easiest distribution racket in the business. West has uncovered all that and he's planning to watch each shop, and to hold the key men when they leave. Anyone who can't produce an alibi for last Monday afternoon between four and six o'clock will be under suspicion, and some of them will crack. You're through—but I'm the only one who knows where you are. You can't stop West picking up the killers, but you can save yourself—if you've got any sense."

"Try and make yourself clearer."

"If I walk out of this place with Ruth Endicott, I'll forget I came here." Owen stood back, now, sneering. "If I don't, West will get a message which I left for him. I can pick it up myself, or he'll pick it up—and don't ask me where it is, because nothing would make me talk, Cockleshell. I'll do a deal —Ruth in return for keeping my mouth shut about this place."

"If I arranged this, how could I be sure that you would keep your word?" demanded Shell.

"Listen to me," said Owen, "I'm a copper. I'm on the Yard's pay-roll—getting the miserly fifteen quid a week they expect a Detective Constable to live on. But it's a job. And I can pick up a lot on the side. I know my way about. I know how to wink at strip-tease houses and whore-shops and gambling hells. There's a lot I can do to pick up the dough on the side, and I could pass on a lot of information to people like you. But if I took Ruth out and ran to West—what would happen to me?"

The woman said: "Very soon you would get your throat cut."

"That's how I see it, too," Owen said, and he moistened his lips. "I wouldn't survive another month. And I'm booked for a long life. Number One's the important thing to me, with Ruth Endicott running close. If I get out with her, West can sing for you. When you've settled down again—well, we can work together, can't we? It would be a mutual benefit society. But don't make any mistake, I've planned it so that if I don't get away with the girl, West will know about this place, and you'll be on the run."

Owen stopped, and wiped the sweat off his forehead with his sleeve. Shell looked at Fats, who made no move to touch his chin.

"For a person with a big reputation," Owen said, "you take a long time to make up your mind."

Very slowly, Shell said: "I've made up my mind, Owen. I don't trust you. I never trust a policeman unless I know it's safe. But I'll make you an offer."

"I've told you my terms."

"That's right. You've made yourself very clear. Now I'll make myself clear. You can leave here, but keep away from West; tell him nothing. I'll send any unreliable men from the shops, so that West won't be able to make them talk. If he stays away from here, you can have the woman in the morning. You simply have to prove to me you haven't lied. You can go free, and do what you like. If you tell West about this place, you'll have your throat cut before the month is out. If we're raided this evening or during the night, the Endicott woman will have hers cut."

She paused.

"You can take your choice, Owen. It's up to you. I can use a man on the inside at the Yard. It would be worth five thousand a year, and pickings—wouldn't it, Fats?"

She paused. Fats cleared his throat and said: "It certainly would."

"So take it or leave it," Shell said; and quite suddenly she laughed. It had a pleasant tinkling sound. "All my shop raiders will leave Cockell's stores by half past four, so West will be too late to pick up anyone who can talk. And if West or any more police come near here, I shall get plenty of warning. I'll go down to the air raid shelter and I'll take pleasure in personally cutting Ruth Endicott's throat. Then my assistants and I will use a way of escape that neither you nor West will think of. You haven't a chance if you're lying, Owen. But if you play fair with me, you'll be all right and so will the girl."

. . . . .

Owen heard the woman's suave voice, and took in the words, but for the moment did not take in all their significance. Only one thing really seemed important. West had given him an hour. That was all the time he had to save Ruth's life.

He did not give his own a thought.

He heard Shell say, in the same suave way: "All right, Fats. Owen can go."

XXIII

RAID

APPLEBY slapped his straw boater on the side of his head at a deliberately rakish angle, and looked at Roger, who was at the wheel of his car, pulled up at a corner not far from the main road to Epping Forest. The radio reports kept coming in, and he could pick out some of the messages clearly. Roger was staring straight ahead of him, at a glade in the forest; his hands were firm on the wheel.

"Don't take it so hard, Handsome," Appleby said. "Men have d-d-died in the way of duty before. You ought to b-b-be more objective. I think I'm disappointed in you."

Roger said wryly:

"So now you hate me, too."

Appleby looked startled. "Eh?" Then he grinned. "Oh— my wife hated you. I remember. No, Handsome, b-b-but you take this too hard. Of course I'm sorry for the poor k-k-kid, but she isn't sorry for herself. That's one of the things it's easy to forget—the d-d-dead don't grieve."

"Maybe not," said Roger, and put a cigarette to his lips, flicked a lighter, and blew smoke out of the open window. "Bella Dawson may be one of many, but there wasn't a thing I could do to stop it happening. I *could* have kept Owen and this Endicott girl out of danger."

"Now get rid of this 'I've sent 'em to their death' complex," urged Appleby. "Every serving officer who ever sent a patrol out on duty would feel that, if there was any reason in it. Forget it, Handsome."

Roger sent smoke curling towards the window.

Appleby went on: "I'll tell you one thing. I've discovered the difference between me and a detective, and you've done the teaching."

"Someone had to," Roger said.

Appleby chuckled.

"All right, all right, I suppose I asked for that. But it's a fact. I don't mind admitting that I have long since l-l-laboured under an illusion. I thought I was the c-c-c-clever one, and you chaps were limping along in the rear. The way some of your senior officers slap their flat feet over clues is b-b-beyond words. A lot of coppers destroy twice as many clues as they find. But there's more to detecting and police work than seeing the injuries and making deductions from them," went on Appleby, and now he sounded really earnest. "Take this j-j-job. The police organisation is unbelievable. The knowledge of people and places, the split-second timing, all that kind of operational activity shakes me. I couldn't begin to handle it, but you're on top of the situation all the time. Every one of those shops watched, a cordon round Forest Ley so cleverly done that no one would know it existed—this is the real stuff of police work. I've never seen it demonstrated so perfectly before. Object lesson, in fact."

Roger said: "It will be, if it works."

"Your big mistake," said Appleby, "and it's probably your heaviest cross in life. You judge only by results. Most unscientific. You should judge a man by the results he gets measured against his ability to get results."

"Should I?" asked Roger, and shifted his position. "Dan, there's a missing piece to this puzzle. There nearly always is. It's the answer to a question I asked early on—and haven't been able to answer yet. Why was Mabel Stone murdered? Why was the man who went into her shop ready to kill? That answer's around somewhere."

He broke off, as he heard his name called clearly. He flicked on his radio and said: "West speaking—over." There was a pause, before *Information* said:

"Fourteen men have left Cockell shops, sir. Seven have been traced to the hostel at Lambeth run by Mrs. Stone. Five other assistants are heading in the Lambeth direction."

Roger said very slowly: "That's exactly what I wanted to hear. All instructions still stand—don't stop anyone going in, but if any of the men come out, hold them. Make sure that our men aren't likely to be identified."

"We've taken care of that."

"Good," said Roger. "Good." He flicked off, and pushed his hat to the back of his head, so far that it fell off on to the seat beside him. He tossed his cigarette out of the window. There was more alertness in his manner as he sat up. "Well, we look as if we've got them on the run."

He was smiling very tautly.

Appleby said: "Don't look so damned smug. What was that about Mrs. Stone running a hostel?"

"Jim Stone's mother," said Roger, very softly. "Jim Stone's mother. It's beginning to make sense. I think I can see the answer to that question, Dan."

"Then pass it on!"

Roger said: "Oh, not yet. The learned pathologist needs a few more lessons in assessing and interpreting apparently irrelevant and non-medical facts." He was very tense. "Jim Stone, a strapping, well-educated, intelligent man who had no time for his mother, who in turn had none for his wife. You deduced a lot from Mabel Stone's body and her blood, but there was one thing you heard about but didn't interpret. Her background. Very humble, and near-Cockney, making a queer marriage—Public school and a poor part of London. Dan——"

"You smooth Smart Alec," Appleby protested. "Wait a minute. I'm getting the wavelength."

"After I'd tuned you in," said Roger. "But what does it matter who tuned you in? Cockell died two years or so ago, leaving his widow the sole beneficiary—not his son. Why not?" When Appleby didn't answer, Roger went on: "Supposing he was Mrs. Stone's son by a first marriage."

Appleby breathed: "Damn it, this isn't deduction, this is sheer guess work."

"Reasonable deduction," Roger insisted. "Very reasonable deduction indeed." He flicked on the radio again, called *Information*, and went on: "I want Jim Stone *alias* Simpson taken to Forest Ley as soon as I can. I'll be at the by-road where I arranged to see Owen. Make it snappy."

"Right away, sir."

"Thanks," said Roger. He flicked off, moved his hand from the radio to the ignition key, switched on the engine, then let in the clutch. "Want to come any further?"

"Try leaving me behind," said Appleby.

"There'll come a time when I'll have to," Roger said, "and I don't mean maybe. When I say you stop here, that's where you stop—I can take chances with myself and my own men but not with Home Office pathologists."

"I'll be good," promised Appleby. "What's your next move?"

"To close in on Forest Ley," Roger said. "We can't be sure what——"

He broke off as a motor-cyclist swung round the corner, engine roaring; the man seemed to lean too far over to one side, and likely to crash, but he straightened up. Appleby said: "*What's this?*" in a tone of sharp alarm, as if he feared an attack by one of the shop raiders. The motor-cycle hurtled closer, and as it drew level with the car the rider flicked something towards it. Appleby cried: "*Look out!*" and ducked. A small box fell into Roger's lap. The motor-cycle roared past, and Roger sat grinning at the pathologist.

"You need training," he said. "You need to judge these things by their potential, not by success or failure." He held a match box in his hand. "A present from young Owen," he went on, and there was deep satisfaction in his voice. "Yes, that was Owen." He opened the match box, and inside were some pebbles and a folded note. As he smoothed this out, Appleby leaned over to see it—a red-faced Appleby.

The note read:

Woman named Shell (Cockleshell) at the house. One man at least upstairs. She nearly fell for my spiel—she's come three-quarters of the way. She, Slessor and several men are at Forest Ley. Give me five minutes' start—R.E. is in the air raid shelter at F.L. and I'd like to get her out.

Appleby said slowly: "A woman."

"Owen's good," Roger said.

"Another thing you chaps need is cold courage," said Appleby heavily.

"Nothing cold about Owen," said Roger, and he flicked on his radio again. "West calling all cars and patrols concentrated in the Epping Forest area. West calling . . ." he repeated the call, and then went on: "In five minutes from now move in on suspect's house. Remember suspect is not alone and is likely to be armed. Allow a motor-cyclist on a red Indian machine to enter drive of Forest Ley without hindrance."

"You see what I mean?" said Appleby. "It's a matter of timing. Seriously think it will all be over in half an hour?"

"We'll either have Shell and Slessor, or they'll have fooled us," Roger said. He beckoned to a plain-clothes man who was in the guise of a window cleaner. "When the man Simpson or Stone comes, have him brought to Forest Ley at once, will you?"

"Yes, sir," the man promised.

.   .   .   .   .

Cyril Owen tossed the message in the match box through the window of West's car, and opened the throttle so that his machine surged forward. He turned another corner, leaning over as if he were racing, and then straightened up on a main road. He was quite sure that now Shell would know what was happening, and he was equally sure that Shell meant exactly what she had said about Ruth. Time was of vital importance. Owen raced the machine along towards Forest Ley.

Not far away from the house, a telephone wire was being serviced. Further along, a postman was delivering letters. Within reach were telegraph "boys", electricity repair men, and private motorists, none of them noticeable, all ready to move in at a signal. Owen slowed the machine down, and approached Forest Ley more cautiously. No one was at the front gate. When he turned in, he saw that the Austin was already at the front door, moved from the spot where he had seen it before.

Fats was coming out of the door, bustling.

He stopped at the sight of Owen, and Owen heard him call out: "*There's Owen!*" Owen had a moment of dread, that he was too late, that the other woman had finished what she had threatened to do with Ruth; there was only one way to find out. He gave the accelerator all he could. The motor-cycle raced along the drive, over the grass, then between the garage and the house itself, towards the air raid shelter.

He saw Shell on the back lawn, framed with crimson ramblers. At the roar of the motor-cycle engine, she spun round like a dancer. Owen saw the gun in her hand, and knew exactly what she intended to do.

Fats came running forward. Slessor appeared behind Shell. The first bullet came with a sharp report, cracking into the mudguard.

·   ·   ·   ·   ·

In the darkness of the air raid shelter, Ruth Endicott was sitting against the wall, her legs stretched out, her body chilled with terror.

She was over the panic-stricken fear of the darkness, but was still terribly afraid. Little creaking noises were nearby, scaring her. She kept hearing rustling sounds, as if there were rats down here; and she was listening all the time for footsteps, for the threatened return of Fats and the other man with him. She had lost all count of time; it might have been an hour, it might have been three or four since she had been thrown in there. She knew that it was a small place, that there was another door at the far end, and that the air was fresh; that was all.

Now and again, a picture of Cy formed itself in her mind, with all that he had come to mean. She kept telling herself that he couldn't have made love to her simply to make her talk, but she was afraid that it was true.

She was utterly helpless.

When Fats started to question her, she would not be able to tell him what he wanted to know. No one would believe her when she said she knew nothing—and Fats would try to make her change her mind.

Her wrist and her arm still ached from the twisting which he had given them.

It was so dark—so frightening—so terrifying.

Then she heard the sound of a motor-cycle. She did not know how near it was, although it seemed to be coming nearer. One moment there had been absolute silence which seemed likely to go on for ever, then suddenly the staccato beat of the engine. It *was* getting louder. She thought that she heard a man cry out, but could not be sure. The roar now seemed to fill the little air raid shelter, there were quivering sounds which got deeper and deeper. She heard a loud report, of something like a backfire; and suddenly realised that it was a shot. The noise was absolutely deafening. It seemed as if the machine were going to crash into the shelter itself.

She heard a rending, thunderous crash, the loudest sound she had ever heard, and there were other sounds, as of falling stones or bricks. Then came more shots, and at last, Cy's voice:

"Ruth, are you all right? Ruth!"

"Cy!" she screamed. "Cy, I'm in here! Cy, are you there? *Are you there?*"

He said: "Keep quiet and don't worry. Don't worry at all. I'll keep 'em away from you."

"Cy, are you all right?"

"I'm fine," he said. "I'm fine. I——"

Then his voice broke off, and she heard another sharp report, undoubtedly a shot; and she heard him exclaim, as if in pain.

XXIV

SACRIFICE

"All right," Roger said into the radio telephone. "Move in now." He flicked the mouthpiece off, and concentrated on his driving, startling Appleby by the way he took the next corner. "Owen's got in there. Now we've got to get him out." He swung round another corner, and a motor-cyclist who looked like a post office telegraph "boy" called out:

"Follow me!"

Appleby was nursing his straw hat.

"How f-f-far is it?" he demanded. "Time enough to k-k-kill me?"

"Just hold tight," Roger said. He felt both excitement and satisfaction, and did not realise that Appleby was staring at him, seeing that excitement in his eyes, knowing that the thing Roger West really thrived on was positive action; if there was a fight, he hated not to be able to be in it, and at moments like this would rather have had Owen's rank than his own.

The motor-cyclist "boy" turned a corner; when they swung round, Roger saw other cars and vans drawn up across the road, blocking the approach to and all escape from Forest Ley.

Roger pulled up at the side of the road, got out, and spoke as Appleby started to follow.

"You stay here. Your job comes later." He began to run towards the drive of Forest Ley, and a man caught up with him. "How are things? Owen all right?"

"I shouldn't think he stands a chance," the man said. "He's crashed his machine at the entrance to the air raid shelter. Three men are trying to get there. They——"

The crack of a shot came clearly.

Roger turned into the drive, and saw several plain-clothes policemen by the side of the house, one man on top of the garage. As he reached the nearest man, the man on the roof warned:

"Careful, super!"

Roger called up: "What's the position?"

"There are two men with revolvers at the air raid shelter. Whenever we show our noses they shoot. Can't tell you what's going on below them. I've got some tear gas here. If I could throw a shell into the mouth of the shelter it might do some good. Angle's a bit awkward, though."

Roger said: "Yes." He pushed his way towards the corner of the house. As he reached it, a shot barked and a bullet chipped pieces off the brick. The man on the roof of the garage said:

"I warned you, sir."

Roger called: "You over there! It's a waste of time. We've got all your men, and you can't get away."

No one answered, no-one fired. There was a shuffling sound, as if a long way off; Roger believed that it was coming from the shelter itself.

"Other end of the garden covered?" he demanded.

"Yes, sir."

"And the approaches to all neighbours' houses, both sides in both roads?"

"Yes, sir."

"Good," said Roger. "Hand me down one of those gas shells."

"But, Mr. West——"

"Hand one down," said Roger. "Don't throw the damned thing." He watched the top of the air raid shelter closely, saw only the dark approach to the steps leading down, and could not be sure whether anyone was still there or not; but he was sure of one thing. Young Owen was there with the Endicott girl, and they had to be rescued.

If they were alive.

He looked back towards the front of the house, and saw men moving about; then one man appeared at the gate, thrusting ahead of the others.

This was the bearded Simpson, *alias* Stone, *alias*—whom?

The man came towards him, and Roger waited, grim-faced. A hammering sound came from the air raid shelter, as if a door were being battered down.

"Is your mother Mrs. Cockell, sometimes known as Mrs. Stone?"

Stone answered gruffly:

"Yes." After a pause, he went on: "She used her original married name—my father's name."

"Listen, Stone," Roger said, "there's a police officer and the woman Endicott, down in that air raid shelter. Your mother is shooting at anyone who goes near. Can she escape through the other end of the shelter?"

Stone said: "Not if you've surrounded the house behind this."

"She thinks she can get out, then," Roger said. "She'll probably kill the prisoners on her way. Would she kill you?"

"I'll find out," Stone said in a hard voice.

He went towards the entrance to the air raid shelter, calling in a clear voice:

"Mother, you've got to give yourself up. You and Slessor and everyone there. You've got to give yourself up."

Then, after a pause, he called again:

"Mother, this is Jim. You've got to give yourself up."

He was half-way to the air raid shelter when the woman appeared, as if she had to make sure that the approaching man was her son. As her head showed above the steps, Roger ran forward from a standing start, and hurled the tear gas shell over Stone's head, and into the entrance of the air raid shelter.

.   .   .   .   .

Ruth heard only odd little sounds after the first shot, and she kept crying Cy's name, but he did not answer, and there were no more sounds of footsteps. She pressed against the locked door, longing for word from him, but everything was silent, and his voice stilled.

Then other voices broke the quiet, footsteps sounded; and the woman Shell asked clearly:

"Is he dead?"

"Can't be alive after that lot." That was Fats. "But he's blocking the entrance, and we can't get in."

"Can't you clear the wreckage away?"

"We'll need ten minutes," said the second man; it was the handsome Slessor. "The police will be here if we don't keep them off."

"Only one of us can work down here," said the woman. "You move the machine and get that door open. Slessor and I will keep the police off."

Ruth pressed against the door, eyes tightly closed, hating what she had learned. At first the sounds outside meant nothing to her, but soon she understood what was happening. One man, Fats, was moving aside the wreckage so that he could open the door. So they needed to come into the air raid shelter to escape from the police. Once they saw her they would kill her; terror drove away all other emotion. She stood away from the door. She heard the metallic sounds of the wreckage being moved, and once Shell came near and asked:

"How much longer?"

"Nearly through," Fats said.

Ruth stood in the darkness, until suddenly the light went on —the blessed light, she would have thought only a short while ago. It showed the bare cement walls, the oddments about the shelter, the far doorway; and she realised that the other door was the way of escape for these people. They would kill her for the sake of killing, she had no doubt about that.

She heard a different sound, a sharp click; and a moment later she heard the door begin to open. Suddenly, wildly, she turned round, snatched up a chair, and smashed the lights; and darkness fell in here. She heard Fats exclaim. She saw a faint light filter in, but it was still very dark. She heard the man breathing, then heard the creak of the door as it opened, and saw the shape of Fats, vague and shadowy. She brought the chair down on his head and shoulders, heard him cry out, and then heard men's voices, and shouting.

Fats was lying in a heap in the doorway.

A man called: "Mrs. Endicott, are you there?"

She began to cry.

.   .   .   .   .

Roger forced his way past the tear gas cloud, through the wreckage of the motor-cycle and over a man's huddled body. Other police were following him. Already Shell, a dark man, and Slessor, had been taken prisoner, and Stone had gone back to the road. Roger shone a torch round the cellar, and saw Ruth Endicott's bowed figure close to the wall. He went towards her, put his arms round her, and heard her saying to herself: "He's dead, he's dead."

  .   .   .   .   .

Appleby said: "He's not dead yet, Handsome. If we can get him to hospital qu-qu-quickly, and send for MacKenzie, he'll stand a chance. He didn't do himself any good c-c-crashing the machine here, and he got a bullet in his head, but— well, I've told you."

Appleby was looking pale.

"We'll fix it," Roger said, and turned to Ruth Endicott, who was standing looking at Owen's unconscious figure. "You heard that—he's got a chance." He raised a hand to some local men, and saw an ambulance already on its way into the drive. It would still be touch and go.

Roger began to give orders.

He finished his inspection of the air raid shelter an hour later. The second door wasn't a normal second exit, but led to another deeper shelter at a lower level, and to a tunnel which ran beneath the garden of the house behind Forest Ley. There had been good reason for Mrs. Cockell to believe that she had a chance to escape; she might have done, but for her son and Owen. It would do no harm to let Ruth Endicott believe that her own desperate attack on Fats had made quite sure that the others were captured.

When the ambulance had gone, and the prisoners from Forest Ley had been taken off, Roger and Appleby, with an Epping Superintendent, met Jim Stone in the library at the back of the house.

"Yes, I'll tell you all I can now," Stone said, still gruffly. "It goes back a long way, but I'll make it short. My father was as honest as they come, but he died when I was a kid. My mother married Cockell, who made a fortune out of war-time profiteering, and handling stolen goods. When I realized it, I walked out on them. When he died, my mother tried to make peace, but I'd married Mabel by then, and my mother didn't like her. She wanted me to leave her." Stone paused, as if to control his voice. "Cockells' shares were owned by a syndicate at that time, I thought my mother had been bought out, but in fact she retained a controlling interest. She said she didn't. Her original job had been managing the hostel—before she married Cockell—and it seemed natural that she should take that on again.

"She wanted me to go into Cockells, and I wouldn't. She thought it was because of Mabel. You kept asking if anyone had reason to want my wife dead, and the true answer was, yes—my mother had.

"But I couldn't be sure," Stone continued, heavily.

"After I bought that little shop in Whitechapel, I started investigating, and soon recognised Fats as a man who had worked with my father. I found out that he lived at the hostel. By that time I was beginning to fear the truth—that my mother had planned Mabel's murder. Did—did she?".

"I'm afraid she did," Roger answered quietly. "We picked Slessor up, and he's made a full statement. Your mother wanted Endicott dead because he was blackmailing her. She gave him the job of killing your wife first, and then had him killed because he could have given the whole game away."

Stone said: "Yes. Yes, I know. It was the shells I found at Endicott's place which told me. My stepfather had always called my mother Shell, and shells had been used as an identification sign among the criminals who worked for him. But I didn't *know* she was involved," Stone went on. "I was afraid that she was, but didn't know for certain. I just had to try to find out for myself."

.   .   .   .   .

It was a little after eight o'clock that night when Roger got back to the Yard. He found Hardy still at his desk, looking tired, but brisk enough and immaculate.

"Evening, Handsome," he said with unusual affability. "Very nice job."

"In its way," Roger said.

"Twenty-six men arrested at the Lambeth hostel," said Hardy, "and several of them have broken down now they know they haven't a chance. They worked at Cockell's shops normally, went out on these special jobs, and did exactly what you always believed. Two of them say that some were being trained for bigger jobs—banks, wage snatches, that kind of thing."

Roger said: "It had to grow. You couldn't organise a thing like that and not extend the range—it had to start losing efficiency or increase it, and Shell Cockell had the organising mind."

"Where is she?"

"Across at Cannon Row," Roger said. "She hasn't said a word, but Slessor can't stop talking. Fats and a man named Rawson are the same. Not that they've got anything more to tell us; once we'd made sure it was Mrs. Cockell, the rest looked after itself." He dropped on to the arm of a chair. "Any news about Owen?"

"The operation is taking place now."

Roger said: "There's a man we need badly, but Appleby doubts whether he'll be fit enough to come back on the force, even if he lives. If ever there was a case for the George Medal, this is it. He drove his machine full force into the air raid shelter to block the approach to it. If he hadn't, we might have lost out." Roger pushed his hand through his hair, and forced a laugh. "Well, we didn't lose anybody. You don't need a formal report now, do you?"

"Just wanted to hear that you were all right," said Hardy. "You go home. By the way, where's this Endicott woman?"

Roger said, half smiling: "Dr. Appleby took her under his wing. She's at his place. Best thing for her." He stood up, and said: "Good night, Commander," and walked slowly back to his own office, looked round, then went out.

He reached home a little after nine o'clock. The boys were in front of a television set, watching a thriller, while Janet was doing some ironing, and looking at the picture from time to time. Roger said: "I'll go into the front room and have a drink." He turned round, but Martin leaned forward, switched off the television, and said:

"We don't really want that."

"Of course we don't," agreed Richard, and they looked eagerly at their father. "How did it go, Dad?"

"Most of it, very well," replied Roger. "The rest—well, I'll know in the morning."

In fact he knew as early as half past six, when the telephone bell rang. He turned over in bed to pluck up the receiver, felt Janet start, and heard Appleby say:

"Handsome, you can stop worrying."

"Owen?"

"Yes. They got the bullet out. He'll survive, unless he has real bad luck. I've told this young woman here, and she can't stop crying."

"She will," said Roger, softly. "She will."

     ·   ·   ·   ·   ·

Ruth did stop crying six months later, when Owen came out of hospital, and married her. Owen had already resigned from the force, for Jim Stone had inherited his mother's shares and had given him a block in Cockell's Limited. He was already plunging himself into the business.

By then Mrs. Cockell, Slessor and Fats had been hanged.

By then, too, Owen had been cited for the George Medal.

Roger West would never forget the adoration in Ruth Owen's eyes when she looked up at her husband after they had come away from the investiture.

THE END

1636

25¢ for 3 days
5¢ Per Day